"Shhh. Easy," Stick said, low and soft in my ear. He'd felt my body tense at the flashbulbs.

His arm snaked around my waist, pulling me even closer. And damn, but my hand slid up and around his neck.

He typically wore his longish hair loose. About chin length, it was wavy and a light brown, but with some natural highlights that women would pay top dollar for in a salon. Tonight he had it slicked back and in a small club of a ponytail, which just brushed the collar of his tux. And now just brushed the back of my hand as I laid it at the back of his neck.

"Wanna give 'em a show?" he whispered in my ear, then placed a soft, chaste kiss on my forehead.

I looked up at him, and his eyes dropped to my lips, relaying his idea to me. I weighed the options in my head—would it be prudent to have the press see me kiss a boy on the dance floor? A boy that wasn't crusty Edgar Prescott?

No. It would be just jumping from the frying pan to the fire. If I was going to be thrown into this world—and it looked like I hadn't really been given a choice—I was going to do it on my terms. Dictate as much as possible in a world where I had no power.

"Better not," I said, meeting his eye. And then—and I swear it wasn't my intention—my gaze dropped and I looked at his lips. He had a very nice mouth, with full lips. I didn't know that I'd ever seen Stick smile. And just as I was thinking that thought, his mouth lifted into a wide—and oh-so naughty—grin. I looked up to his eyes, and they were staring down at me. Mischief and… something else, something very raw, shining through.

"When have you ever done the smart thing, Jane Winters?" he said as he bent and kissed me.

OTHER TITLES BY
MARA JACOBS

The Worth Series
(Contemporary Romance)
Worth The Weight
Worth The Drive
Worth The Fall
Worth The Effort
Totally Worth Christmas

Freshman Roommates Trilogy
(New Adult Romance)
In Too Deep
In Too Fast
In Too Hard (coming soon)

Anna Dawson's Vegas Series
(Romantic Mystery)
Against The Odds
Against The Spread

Blackbird & Confessor Series
(Romantic Mystery)
Broken Wings

Countdown To A Kiss
(A New Year's Eve Anthology)

IN TOO
FAST

Freshman Roommates, Book Two

MARA JACOBS

Published by Copper Country Press, LLC
©Copyright 2014 Mara Jacobs
Cover design by Mara Jacobs

ISBN: 978-1-940993-95-9

For more information on the author and her works, please
see www.marajacobs.com

For Every Great
Enemies To Lovers
Romance

ONE

I spent my whole life trying to be in the driver's seat.
And then I got behind the wheel.

MY FATHER STOOD about ten feet away from me. Or about seven bridesmaids away, smiling his father-of-the-bride smile for the wedding photographer. His arm around his daughter—the bride, my older half-sister—standing next to him.

"Bridesmaid on the end. Smile, please. Happy thoughts," the photographer coaxed, and I realized he was talking to me.

I flashed my brightest smile. The happy thought that went through my mind was that of the photographer bursting into flames and this whole charade finally being over. He took a few more shots and then motioned the bridal party away and called out his next setup. "Bride's side, immediate family only, please."

I left the altar area and walked with the other bridesmaids—none of whom had said more than three words to me this whole, excruciatingly long weekend—toward the back of the church sanctuary. I couldn't get out of there quick enough, but the other bridesmaids stopped only a few rows past where the photographer was set up in the middle of the center aisle.

The same aisle I'd marched down just over an hour ago

when my half-sister, Betsy Stratton, married Jason Bohnner III.

It might not have been so bad if it was the type of processional where your corresponding groomsman walked you down the aisle. But Betsy chose the route where each bridesmaid walked down by herself, meeting up with their guy at the altar.

You could have heard a pin drop before my entrance, while the other girls walked down the aisle, accompanied by a tasteful—in a sea of tasteful, this wedding—harpist. Not so when I entered the church. Ever hear a swarm of locusts off in the distance but heading your way? Me neither (not many locust invasions at my oh-so-posh Maryland college), but I imagined that was what the low hum in the very crowded church sounded like when I began my procession.

But I held my head high, pasted on a smile, straightened my shoulders, flipped back my totally awesome hair (my mother sent me to her DC stylist last weekend—begrudgingly, after she realized no way in hell would she be permitted to accompany me to this wedding) and pretended I didn't hear a thing and that they were all just jealous.

Like I've been doing most of my eighteen years.

Hey, you tell yourself something long enough, you start to believe it's true.

The other bridesmaids all took seats, their attention on the front of the altar, where the Stratton family—plus their newest addition, Jason—were gathering for the family shot. Not being an emotional cutter (or any other kind, for that matter) I turned and started to make my way to the back of the church only to hear, "Jane, wait."

If it were Betsy's voice, or even my father's, I would pretend I didn't hear and keep walking. But it was Caroline Stratton, Betsy's mother, my father's ex-wife, who called to me, and so I stopped and turned around to see her motioning for me to join them at the altar.

As I walked back toward the group, I caught the look that passed between Betsy and her older brother—my half-brother (yeah, totally confusing)—Joseph Stratton, Jr.

Joey, to his friends. I didn't consider myself amongst that group. When I did have to talk to him—which was not often—I called him Joseph. He'd never corrected me.

The look between Betsy and Joey only lasted a second, was completely silent, but could be summed up like this:

Betsy: Are you effing kidding me? I invited her to the wedding because Mom and Dad made me. I even made her a bridesmaid because Daddy is paying for the whole thing and said I had to. But the family photos? Really?

Joey: Give her an inch…just like her mother.

Some might say I was being paranoid, that you couldn't get all that from a simple look.

But I've been deciphering looks between this family for years. And just because I was paranoid doesn't mean they weren't out to get me.

Even though they've tried to make me feel like shit for years (though even when they succeeded, I never gave them the satisfaction of knowing it), I do kind of understand Betsy and Joey hating me so much.

Betsy was ten and Joey twelve when I was born. It was a year or so later when their parents split up, Joseph Sr. leaving the house. Never having had a father in the house, I couldn't relate to one leaving, but my friends who went through their parents' divorce said it totally sucked. I believed them.

Given Joey and Betsy's hatred of me from ever since I could remember, I *really* believed them.

"It's okay, Caroline," I said as I got closer to the family. The photographer was positioning them, then stepping back to his camera, then back to them.

She's been having me call her Caroline ever since I can remember. I only call her Mrs. Stratton when I'm speaking about her to my mother. And only then to piss off my mother. Mrs. Stratton is who my mother thought she'd become someday.

Yeah, right. Keep dreaming, Mom.

The crazy thing is, she does…keeps dreaming about it, I mean.

"Jane," Caroline said again. "We'd like you in the photo. You're family."

I dutifully headed to the altar, standing next to my father. We're a striking bunch. My father, now in his early sixties, has aged very well. He's still movie-star handsome. He could be played in the movie version of his life by a slightly older George Clooney.

Caroline's life showed on her face. The cheating husband, public divorce, years of cancer treatments followed by long remissions; they all showed. She looked tired, and a little on the thin side, but was still a handsome woman, and had probably had some stylists work with her today, because she was totally put together. In particular, her shoes: totally killer sling-backs with beading at the peek-a-boo toe that matched her dress.

Betsy and Joey are both white-blonde with clear blue eyes. They look like their mother. I have my father's coloring, darker hair and green eyes. It was very much an "us" and "them" family in looks. And pretty much everything else too. Though I have my own "me" and "him" relationship with my father.

I stood with my "family"—such as it was—and smiled.

I did it because Caroline Stratton was one woman I couldn't pull any crap with. She was…*stately*…was the term they used in the political world. And this woman could have curled up and died long ago, and I don't mean just from the cancer.

No, she took a lot of shit over the years—mostly at the

hands of my mother and father—and came out a class act. Pride intact.

That was going to be me.

Again, I pushed back my shoulders, flipped my hair and tilted my head just a bit to the right; the pose I knew made me look my best. And I smiled like I'd just slept with the hottie professor I'd been trying to bag all semester.

These shots would probably be on the cover of *People*. At the very least they'd be all over the web, and I'd be damned if I looked the part of castoff, bastard daughter.

Even if that was what I was.

TWO

✦✦✦

I WAS THE BABY that brought down the president. Well, he wasn't the president yet, but he was the front-runner on the election trail. Then he hooked up with my mother, got busted for the affair (did I mention he was married for, like, a zillion years and his wife had cancer?), denied being my father and dropped out of the presidential race. His wife divorced him a year later. He finally admitted to being my father, after DNA tests proved it, but his political career was totally shot.

Yeah, total douche, my dad. Biological father. Sperm donor. Whatever.

But he's filthy rich, which was a good thing for me.

And for my mother, who was probably still sucking money out of him. Don't ask, don't tell was my motto on that one.

I rode to the reception at the Chesney Marriott with my father, just the two of us in the humongous limo. The other bridesmaids rode with the groomsmen, bottles of champagne already flowing. I was not asked to join them, nor did I ask to be included.

Standing up for my sister at the altar, being in the photographs, not causing a stink in any way—my job was done. I wasn't really needed anymore, so I sat back in the seat, kicked off the God-awful pumps Betsy insisted that we wear, and stared out the window as we made our way from the church to the Marriott. I resisted the urge to pull my phone out of my bag and text my roommates. I knew that drove my dad crazy, and normally I'd do it just to tweak him, but he'd had a crappy day too, so I left it alone.

"How's your mother, Jane?" my father asked me, no real concern in his voice. Just making conversation. I knew he was thinking about Caroline, not my mother. From what I understood, he and Caroline didn't see each other much anymore, now that Betsy and Joey were grown and had been out of the house for a while. No real reason to communicate.

Seeing each other so much this past week during all the wedding hoopla was probably hard on both of them.

Not that I cared.

"Fine. I guess. I was only home a couple of days before coming here," I answered.

He nodded, as if he'd just remembered I attended college. "Right. And school? How's that going for you?"

"Good."

He looked like he wanted to say more, but let's face it, we've never really had much to say to each other. *"Hey, Pops, sorry Mom wouldn't have that abortion and save you from all that public humiliation! But, hey, if she had, we'd have missed out on all these great daddy/daughter chats."* Uh...no.

We sat in silence for the rest of the drive.

I had to team up with my designated groomsman—Jason's former fraternity brother, Ryan Something-or-other—for our entrance into the ballroom. There was polite applause as the emcee announced us (what were they going to do? stand up and chant "bastard! bastard!"), and we made our way to the head table, which was raised up on a platform of some sort and let us look down on the rest of the gathering.

I did like the idea of that. Looking down on these smug people.

Dinner was a blur, with the two guys sitting on either side of me totally ignoring me and chatting up the girls on their other sides. I had to resist pulling out my phone and texting someone—anyone—just to feel some semblance of control.

But I didn't text anyone. Everyone was waiting for me to do something like that, so I didn't. I ate, and met the eyes of people in the crowd who were staring at me with polite smiles.

Plus, I'd made a deal with Grayson Spaulding to not only be a bridesmaid, but to behave as if I wanted to be there. ("And the Oscar goes to…Jane Winters!")

After dinner, Betsy and Jason danced the first dance together. Then they announced the bride and her father would dance, and the groom and his mother. My father took Betsy and led her into a nice dance to some song that I'd never heard about children growing up. We, the bridal party, made our way to the edge of the dance floor, as we were supposed to do the next dance with our partner.

That would be the last call of duty for Ryan, and then he could hang with all the friends of Jason (of which there were many) or try to hook up with Chrissy, one of Betsy's bridesmaids that he'd been eyeing all night.

Caroline Stratton sat at her table on the edge of the dance floor amongst her friends, and watched her ex-husband dance with their daughter. The table she sat at wasn't far from me, and I was able to see her quite well. She was wearing a tasteful lilac gown and had her hair swept up. Very mother of the bride.

She smiled brightly as she watched Betsy and my father dance. It was her public smile, the one she wore when she knew everyone was watching her—which of course they were—waiting to see her reaction.

I had practiced that smile in the mirror when I was ten years old. I'd had a *People* magazine open next to me on the bathroom counter, opened to the article about my tenth birthday. There was Caroline, walking into the hotel where I was spending the weekend with my father, presents in her arms, her serene smile the only thing she'd give the throng of paparazzi that had camped out in front of the hotel the whole weekend.

Other kids had friends over for their birthdays. Or went to a Chuck E. Cheese's or some other bullshit place.

I'd spent my tenth birthday in a hotel suite in Baltimore, my mother having to leave the room while my father's ex-wife came and brought me a present. It was the first year she hadn't dragged Betsy and Joey with her; they were both in college by then.

"Jaybird Turns Ten!" the headline of the article read. There was a shot of the exterior of the swanky hotel (my father didn't stay in anything less than swanky), the picture of Caroline and a shot of me leaving after the weekend, holding my mother's hand.

I could still remember my mother hissing at me just as we left the safety of the hotel lobby, "Smile, Jaybird—show the cameras what a lovely time you had with your mommy and daddy together."

What the cameras caught, what showed up in the magazines, tabloids and all over the net, was the look of bewilderment and disgust that I shot my mother seconds after she'd said that.

Oh, and I heard about it from her too, after the mags hit the stand. That was why I'd sat in my bathroom for hours on end practicing the smile Caroline Stratton was now pointing toward the happy, dancing couple.

Shortly after that birthday I demanded that everyone call me Jane, not that stupid-ass name my mother gave me, Jaybird. (It had something to do with being free, flying, some New-Agey crap like that.)

I wanted something simple, plain, classic. And I had just read the biography of Miss Jane Pittman, so it had been on my mind. Perfect ten-year-old logic.

I saw flashbulbs going off around me now, and realized that not only was Caroline being studied for her reaction, I was as well. I pretended I didn't see them as I smiled brightly at Betsy and my father (was this the longest song ever, or what?). I looked at them as if I was thinking how happy they were, and how much I would enjoy it being time to dance with my father when I was a bride. More flashbulbs went off.

See what practicing a fake smile in the mirror for years can do for you?

The wedding photographer was one of those with a camera, but there were also a few with press passes on. I assumed they were scheduled to be there, as I'd practically had to give a DNA swab to even get in here with the security my father hired.

Never one to pass up a positive press spin, my father. The master of good press…right up until my birth.

"What a dog and pony show," I heard beside me, and turned to see Joey. He watched Betsy and my dad too. He had a smile plastered on his face, but there was definitely *tone* in his voice.

"Yeah, I guess," I said, all non-committal. Was it a trap? Joey never spoke directly to me unless his mom was standing behind him urging him to do so. Of course, that was several years ago. He was a man now.

Time to put away childish things? Like hating your half-sister for being born?

"You seem to be enjoying it," he said. I wasn't sure if he was commenting on my fabulous acting skills or that he was just surprised that I could possibly be truly enjoying this.

"Yeah. I'd like to thank the Academy…" I said. Out of the corner of my eye I saw him nod. No surprise to him.

"Listen," he said, turning fully to me now. I was relieved to be able to turn to him—turn away from the dance floor. "I'm hitting the road in a couple of days. Heading to Africa—several places in Africa, actually—for a year. I wasn't sure if Dad had told you or not."

I shook my head. My father didn't say much to me in general, and almost nothing about Joey or Betsy. "No, he didn't."

"Figures. Well, I have a great opportunity to work with a relief group in Africa. Given the shit that's about to go down here, I took it. But if you need to talk or anything. I know I was an ass to you when I was a kid, but if you need anything…"

I nodded, touched, then stopped. "What do you mean? What's about to go down here?"

He looked to the dance floor, then back to me, disgust on his face. "Are you serious? No one's told you?" I shook my head. "Dad's going back into politics. He's running for governor of Maryland."

I felt the perfect, normal, out-of-the-spotlight life I'd built for myself being pulled out from under me.

THREE

I WAS A FRESHMAN at Bribury College, a small, elite school between Baltimore and DC. And I loved it there. Loved that I could be just Jane Winters. Loved my roommates Lily and Syd. Loved my classes (as much as you can love college classes).

I should have been spending my break whooping it up with my high school friends back home (not that I had any, having gone to a boarding school for the past four years). But no, I was here at this wedding listening to my half-brother drop a bombshell.

"Are you serious?" I asked. Joey nodded. "Is *he* serious?"

Joey nodded again. "He's putting out *feelers*." He did the air quotes thing around "feelers" and added, "He's invited a bunch of the party's influential people to the wedding."

I didn't say anything. Things made sense now. Why I was here, a bridesmaid. *Step right up, folks, see the elusive, happy political-scandal family. They only appear every millennium. Or every election cycle.*

"What an ego to think the public has forgotten what he did," Joey said.

I saw more flashes out of the corner of my eye and realized the song had—finally, thankfully—ended, and Betsy and my father were making their way to us.

"Forget what he did? Not likely with me standing here."

Joey let out a soft snort. "I know, right?" He seemed to realize that statement could hurt my feelings and added, "No offense."

Really? After all I'd heard in my lifetime, something like that one just rolled off my back. "None taken."

"And now the entire wedding party," the bandleader announced. Betsy had a very prominent band playing *and* a DJ for any intervals. That must have cost a ton.

"That's why the humongo wedding. And the press being here," I said, though I didn't really need to.

"Yep," Joey confirmed. "All for show."

"Well, what wedding isn't, really?" I didn't know why I said that—it almost sounded like I was defending Betsy. Or my father.

Ryan Something-or-other came to take me to the dance floor. "I'll dance with Jane," Joey told him. "You dance with Chrissy."

Ryan couldn't hide the delight from his face—Chrissy was the bridesmaid he'd been hot for. But he shot Joey a look. "I don't know. I don't want the wrath of Bridezilla coming down on me."

"I'll deal with fallout from Betsy," Joey said as he took my hand and led me out onto the dance floor. I saw Betsy do a double take at Joey and me being paired up, but when she saw that Ryan had found Chrissy—that there were no loose ends—she relaxed into the arms of her new husband.

She was probably used to Joey changing things up on her. He went through a bit of a wild phase in his teens. Drinking, expelled from a couple of different prep schools. Acting out, the press called it. I think it pissed my father off—which was probably the point. But I also think it hurt Caroline, which was probably why Joey eventually straightened up, got an Ivy League degree and a good job, and became a model citizen.

But come on. A year in Africa on a relief mission? Uh…no. Not for me. Unless maybe to accompany Brad and Angelina.

"So yeah, the wedding is for show. Betsy actually wanted something small. Just family. Up at the cape." Caroline had a huge place at Cape Cod that had been in her family for generations. I had—for obvious reasons—never been there. That was where Betsy and Joey spent all their summer vacations growing up.

It made sense—Betsy wanting something small. Whereas Joey rebelled, and then accepted the cards he was dealt, and I lived with them my whole life and played them to my advantage, Betsy had gone a different route.

She hated the press, avoided them at every turn. She was a very shy person. She'd had a small, very close circle of friends since her early teens—Jason being amongst them. They had all gone to the same prep school and then Brown.

Of course the size of this wedding would be something she would abhor.

"Why didn't she? Get married at the cape?"

"Dad said he'd pay for everything if she did it up bigger. Including buying her and Jason an apartment in Manhattan."

"Wow," I said, mentally calculating the cost of this wedding and an apartment in New York.

"She and Jason really want to leave their jobs and work in public service, but couldn't do that and live where they wanted to on what they'd probably make…so, she took Dad up on his offer."

"Well…*yeah*," I said as if it was a no-brainer. The look Joey gave me said it wasn't something he would do. "It's not selling out if you wind up doing what you wanted all along anyway," I said.

Joey did a sweeping motion, encompassing the photographers—most of whom had their cameras trained on

Joey and me. "*This* is not what Betsy wanted."

I nodded toward Betsy, who was looking adoringly, happily, at Jason. "Maybe. But she looks pretty happy right now. And they'll be *very* happy in their new apartment."

"It's not that simple, Jane. There's a slippery slope of selling out. You need to hang on to your principles right from the start."

I snorted. "Principles? In the viper's nest we live in?"

"It wasn't always like that."

"Right. Life was Shangri-la until I popped out." I tried to sound normal, but the bitterness in my voice seeped out.

I was right, but Joey tried to hide it. Maybe he had grown up. Maybe I was imagining the subtext of the looks between him and Betsy.

"Not Shangri-la, no. As it turns out, it was all a lie, our happy family. But it's not a lie if you don't know the truth."

"There's some messed-up logic for you," I said.

He shrugged, my hand that rested on his shoulder rising and lowering with his movement. "Politics is full of messed-up logic."

"So are families," I added.

"Yeah," he said, and twirled me around. "Anyway, I'm getting the hell out of Dodge during this circus. Betsy and Jason are going on an extended honeymoon through Europe, then they'll start their new jobs next fall, when the apartment is ready. I'm giving you fair warning—you might want to make yourself scarce for the next six to nine months."

"I'm in the middle of my freshman year at college. How am I supposed to disappear?"

"Right," he said, then looked down at me as if realizing I couldn't live my own life yet, like he and Betsy could. "Can you stay at Bribury during the summer? Take classes?"

"I hadn't planned on it, but I guess I could. Why?"

He shrugged again. "I'm just thinking with Betsy and me away, Dad might come calling on you to hit the campaign trail with him."

Some one-on-one time with my dad—no Betsy or Joey. And most definitely not my mother. Traveling around the country. Stumping, I guess they called it. And then Joey added, "He'll need somebody to trot out to show he has *some* family that still talks to him. That he's not a total douche."

Oh, yeah. Right. I'd be the sacrificial lamb.

My father asked me to dance next, and I waited for him to bring up his going back into politics, but he didn't. He did look over my shoulder whenever he got a chance, probably scoping out where all the reporters and potential bigwigs might be stationed.

Sad, but after our small exchange in the limo on the way to the reception, we really didn't have much more to say to each other. I wanted to bait him about his decision to run for office, but I couldn't really come up with something to say—which was *very* unusual for me.

We danced in silence mostly. He kept an eye on the photographers, and when apparently the moment was right, he smiled down at me. I smiled back at him, like some daughter happy to be dancing with her beloved daddy. Our smiles were such practiced movements it would be hard for anyone to tell just how completely fake it all was.

FOUR

❖

AFTER THE DANCE with my father, I was led to the dance floor by Grayson Spaulding, my roommate Lily's father.

Not asked to dance, mind you, just taken to the dance floor and made to dance with the man that was the brains behind my father's presidential run. And the reason I was even here at the wedding.

"So, governor, huh?" I said to him as he moved me about the dance floor. I found it easier to ask Spaulding about it than my father. I guess that said something about my relationship with my father.

To his credit, Spaulding didn't even appear surprised that I knew about my father's running. Hell, maybe *everybody* knew and I was just, as usual, catching up.

"We're going to need your support for this campaign, Jane," he said to me. He looked me in the eyes for this.

This. This was the difference between Grayson Spaulding and Joseph Stratton. Spaulding knew everybody was watching us, and he kept his eyes on me, seeming oblivious to it all.

My father *needed* to see the people watching him. It was as if he wouldn't believe it otherwise. That need to see the adoration (as it had been in years past) or the curiosity (as it was now).

Spaulding knew it was there, smelled it like a bloodhound,

but didn't need to visually confirm it.

That's why some people needed to run for public office and others were perfectly content to be the man behind the curtain, pulling the levers and making the steam rise.

"We already made our deal, Mr. Spaulding," I said. "Here I am, pretending to be a happy part of the family."

"I think we're to the point where you can call me Grayson, don't you? Typically I'm on a first-name basis with my extortionists."

"I would say your co-conspirator, if anything...Grayson."

A small smile crept across his face as he looked down at me. "I like you, Jane. I'll bet you're good for Lily."

"Wasn't it supposed to be that she'd be good for me?"

He gave an elegant shrug to his shoulder, and I realized the puppet master had strings even I couldn't see.

And I looked for strings at all times, with all people.

"How do you think I'm good for Lily?" I asked, resigned to the fact that this assumption was part of his plan from the beginning.

He studied my face, almost as if wondering if I could handle the truth. His eyes softened just the tiniest bit, and I realized he now knew that, sadly, at almost nineteen, I could handle just about anything.

"It would appear to most people that Lily would be a grounding presence to you, having the upbringing you did."

"You mean having a new-age, gold-digging twit for a mother and a douchebag fame-whore for a father? What about that screams instability?"

He didn't actually roll his eyes at my sarcasm—I would have bet that Grayson Spaulding had never deigned to roll his eyes—but a soft exhale left him, which said he wasn't pleased with my summation. Accurate as it may be.

"But it is also true that you would have a...liberating

effect on Lily. She was truly caught in a 'middle child who feels they must be perfect to be noticed' situation."

Wow. He'd nailed Lily perfectly. And here I'd assumed—and I'm guessing Lily had too—that her father was completely oblivious to her feelings.

"You weren't afraid I'd lead her down the wrong path of… liberation?"

He studied me again, and I felt like he knew every one of my secrets. It was probably how politicians felt when he told them which way he wanted them to vote on a bill or something.

If he even did that sort of thing. It might all be about the campaign to him, not the actual governing. The race itself might be the crack that Grayson Spaulding smoked.

"No. I was not concerned about that, Jane."

"Why not? I've dragged Lily to parties where I've been stinking, falling-down drunk. I've had to send her out of the room while I've banged a guy silly. And have asked her to join me…in both activities."

An exaggeration on all accounts, but he didn't need to know that. Although he probably already did, the all-knowing bastard.

"I appreciate the shock value, Jane. But let's save that for bragging around the cafeteria table, shall we?"

"I don't brag around the cafeteria table," I said, indignant. Sooooo not my style.

"I know," he said with a tiny smile.

I nodded to him, acknowledging that he'd got me on that one. Then decided to tackle the elephant in the room.

"So just how do you see me being of any help to my father's campaign? 'Cause I can only see tabloid headlines and paparazzi camped out in front of my dorm in my future."

He gave the tiniest of head shakes. "That won't happen. We'll make sure that Bribury is off limits."

I imagined that he could probably make that happen.

"What about the tabloid headlines?" I motioned with my chin to the row of approved photographers, and even the people taking photos, and shooting video, with their phones. "Beginning with today's little farce of a happy family."

"That's why we're getting out ahead of it. Of course they're going to dredge it all up again—Joe's affair with your mother, you being born—"

"Him denying he was my father?"

He gave a curt nod, and looked away for a moment. But it was enough.

"Or—wait. Did *you* tell him to deny me? Was that your piece of political strategy?"

It had backfired royally. But it would have taken some of the sting out of knowing that it hadn't been my father's idea to disavow that he'd ever had an affair with my mother and that they'd created me.

"Yes, that was my idea. And I apologize to you for it, though it's a little late."

I studied him, the way he'd studied me so closely a moment ago.

The tiny swelling I'd had for a brief second thinking that my father—though he hadn't stood up to this guy way back then, when he should have—hadn't wanted to deny me sank as I realized the master manipulator I was dancing with was at it again.

"You're lying," I said. Before he could answer me, I continued, "You want me to believe that now so I'll get all warm and fuzzy toward good ol' Joe, but we both know it was his idea to deny the whole thing ever happened. Including me. *Especially* me. I'll bet you even tried to talk him out of it at the time. Am I right?"

God, I desperately wanted to be wrong. How pathetic was

that? Still hungry for crumbs of Daddy's affection even after all these years of knowing I'd never have it.

But I knew I was right.

There was no pity in his eyes (thank God) when he answered me. "Yes." He twirled me a little then—a showy move for someone who left the showy moves to others.

When we came to rest, he said, "You would make a great candidate someday, Jane. I only wish I'd still be in the game then."

"Why? And more importantly, hell no."

He smiled then, a real, genuine smile. It was kind of nice, in a dad sort of way. "Never say never. Especially with your bloodline and connections."

"I don't have any connections."

"Look around you, Jane. This room is filled with your future connections."

"Why do you think I'd be good at this backstabbing, all-for-show world?"

"Because you have your father's charm and your mother's scheming." I recoiled from his words, but he held on to me. "I mean that as a compliment, Jane."

"None taken."

He smiled again.

I shook my head, wanting to shake his words off me.

"That deal you made? So Lily could go on seeing Lucas? That was ballsy and a stroke of genius."

I shrugged. But yeah, I was a little flattered.

"I'd be even more impressed if you told me you'd played it that way from the beginning. If you had Lily make her deal with me, knowing you'd come back and counter with your deal, getting the outcome you wanted."

He gave me too much credit. Plus… "You think this is the outcome I wanted?" I motioned with my chin to the proceedings around us, and down to the bridesmaid's dress I was wearing.

"Perhaps not."

"Besides, I was on board with Lily being away from Lucas. I didn't know at the time…" I stopped. This wasn't really my story to tell to Lily's father.

"Know what?"

What the hell. Lily had taken Lucas home to meet her parents over the holidays, so Spaulding must have seen it too.

"How much he loves her."

He stiffened, but not a flicker of emotion changed on his face. It was an okay face. Kind of average for a dad. Not movie-star handsome like my father, but…pleasant. It certainly didn't show the barracuda of a man that he was.

"You did get that, right?" I asked. "That they're crazy in love? And not just 'teen angst, they'll get over it in a week' kind of love?"

He swallowed, took his time. "Yes. I got that."

"Good for you for admitting it," I said, somewhat surprised that he had. I assumed Grayson would be of the mind that if he didn't acknowledge it, it wasn't true.

"I have found it serves me well to see situations as they truly are, not as I would wish them to be."

"Damn, good line. I'll have to remember that one."

He smiled again. "You can have it—use it at will. What's more, try to live by it."

I thought that was pretty good advice. Advice I was going to take.

"So, back to me and the campaign. Or, in other words, why would you want me within ten feet of it, and why would I bother?"

He liked cutting to the chase; he was that kind of man. And I found I was becoming that kind of woman.

"We'll get out in front of it. We can't hide it—obviously. So instead we use it to our advantage."

"Having a child with your mistress while your wife was undergoing cancer treatments? How the hell do you take advantage of that?" But I knew how before he even said it.

"Because the two people he wronged the most—Caroline by cheating on her, and you by denying you—will have forgiven him and be by his side during his campaign."

"Holy shit, Caroline is willing to do that?"

I'd played my cards wrong, and just the tiniest tic at the corner of his eye alerted me to that fact.

By jumping right to Caroline, it made him think that either I'd do it if Caroline would, or that I found Caroline's involvement more shocking than the idea of helping myself, so maybe I'd be open to the idea.

Damn. And he'd be right, too, if that was indeed what he thought. And it was. I was coming late to the party, but I learned the rules quickly.

I always had.

"I mean, not that I'm willing to…"

He quirked a brow up at me. Yeah, he had me, and he knew that I knew he had me.

I rolled my eyes (*I* wasn't above it) at him. "Whatever. Seriously. Caroline is going to go out and stump for her slimeball ex-husband?"

"She will make herself available as needed for the father of her children."

"Oh. Yeah. Okay, I get it now. She'll toe the line so her kids' father isn't dragged through the dirt. Again."

"Something like that. And, of course, for their legacy."

"Doesn't seem like Joey wants anything to do with that legacy. He's hightailing it to Africa just to get away from it."

Grayson didn't seem all too happy being reminded of

that fact. "Yes, the timing of that trip is…unfortunate. As well as Betsy being in Europe. But we can spin it into something positive."

"Do-gooding runs in the family? Something like that?"

"Jane, you do catch on quickly. It's going to be a pleasure working with you on this."

"Whoa. Haven't agreed to anything yet."

He quirked a brow again.

"Or even begun discussing terms," I added, which garnered me another smile. "Plus, the new semester starts next week." Which, of course, he knew because of Lily. He only nodded. "I don't want to miss school. I'm not going to leave school to get on some campaign bus or anything. I just want to clarify that right now, before we go any further in discussing this whole ludicrous idea."

"I can fix things at Bribury if you're—"

"It's not that I'm afraid I'll flunk freshman courses or anything. I just don't want to…miss out."

He looked at me for a long while, and I looked away, not able to meet his eye. Not wanting him to see how much being Jane Winters at Bribury, where nobody had heard of me, meant to me.

"We'll do most of the prep work these next few months. Announce it. Have interviews done with you, and also Caroline, with friendly journalists. But we'll keep you out of it as much as possible during the school year. During the summer is when we'll use you."

Use me. Yep, that pretty much summed me up. I was used by my mother to try and catch my father. I was used by the opposing party to bring my father down. I was used by the press to sell magazines.

Bribury was immune to all that, so far. I was smart enough to know I wouldn't be able to outrun my parents forever, but longer than freshman year would have been nice.

Okay, time to put on my big-girl panties and make the situation work to my advantage.

Just as I was about to start negotiating in earnest, I saw a man walking along the edge of the dance floor that made me miss a step in the dance.

"What's Montrose doing here?" I asked, and Mr. Spaulding followed my line of vision.

"Billy Montrose went to Brown with Betsy and Jason," he explained.

"Seriously? I didn't see him at the wedding."

"Neither did I. I'm glad he made it to the reception," Spaulding said.

"Why?"

"His star is a bit tarnished, but he was quite the storm in the literary world a few years ago."

"So there would be more 'names' here other than political ones, right?" I asked.

"Doesn't hurt."

I kind of knew Montrose had been a big deal when he'd first published, but how big of a deal could he have been if only some years later he was relegated to guest-teaching Intro to Creative Writing to freshmen at Bribury College?

But damn, he was hot. And I'd had him in my sights since day one.

"Okay," I said to Spaulding. "I'll think about it and get back to you. I'll certainly have some *requests* for my participation."

The song was ending, and I kept watching Montrose move through the group of people at the edge of the dance floor. He stopped to shake hands with one of the groomsmen, another Brown crony.

I broke away from Mr. Spaulding, intending to get Montrose to dance with me. It must be fate that he was at this wedding—an event I in no way wanted to attend. And I wasn't his student anymore, so he couldn't use that rebuff on me as he had the night I'd seen him at a club in Chesney last fall.

And yes, it was not lost on me that this was exactly what my mother had probably done all those years ago—got my father in her sights and went in for the kill.

Regardless, I would make my move.

FIVE

"OH, LOVELY JAYBIRD all grown up. May I have this dance?" some old codger said to me as he stepped in my path.

"Umm, I'm actually—"

"She'd love to dance with you, Edgar," my father said, from, like, out of nowhere. "Jane, you probably don't remember Edgar Prescott. One of my oldest, and most trusted, advisors."

Didn't remember him because surely I'd never met him. This being my "debut" into political society and all.

"No. I'm sorry, I don't recall." I was about to throw some shade, but I could see Grayson watching me from a few feet away. Might as well show him I was capable of cooperation before the negotiations began. I stuck out my hand. "It's a pleasure, sir. Are you enjoying yourself?"

"I'd enjoy myself more if I could spin you around the dance floor, my dear."

Spaulding took a step forward at the same time my father all but pushed me at Prescott. "She'd be delighted, Edgar."

I caught Montrose looking at me. He didn't seem surprised to see one of his students in a bridesmaid's dress at his former classmates' wedding.

I smiled at him and he smiled back, then nodded toward my next dance partner. "Have fun," he mouthed, and I stopped myself before mouthing back to him what I thought of that.

He knew, though, and laughed.

God, he was sexy in a rumpled, tragic-artist kind of way.

"So, Mr. Prescott," I said, as the old man took my hand in his surprisingly strong grip and led me to the far side of the dance floor, which was quickly filling up. "Are you enjoying yourself this evening?"

He stopped at the far corner of the dance floor, almost to the doors that led to the now deserted kitchen.

"It's much better now that I can hold a beautiful girl in my arms," he said, and slid an arm around my waist, lifting up the hand he still held and leading me in the dance.

"That's very sweet," I said, giving him a good smile. Not my best smile, mind you—I still wasn't sure just how powerful ol' Edgar was, though my father's happiness at me dancing with the old fart had been obvious.

He looked around the floor, as did I. We were swallowed up by the dancers, unable to see to the group of people beyond the several couples who encircled us. He seemed pleased by that, and I felt a twinge of unease.

"My God, but you're something," he said, looking down at me. He had to be late seventies or even eighties, but he was still an imposing figure. Not handsome…but imposing.

"Umm…thanks," I said, not really sure it was a compliment. And not really sure he was even directing it at me. He had a glassy look in his eye that made me think either he'd had too much to drink, or was thinking about someone—or some time—other than me. Or both. Either way, he made me start to feel a little uncomfortable.

He was a strong leader on the dance floor, and his grip was equally strong, despite the boniness of the fingers that clutched mine.

He twirled me a couple of times and moved more quickly than I thought he was capable of, until we were off the dance floor and had actually passed through a set of swinging doors.

I was reminded of all those historical romance novels and books where the dashing rogue steers the breathless debutante off the dance floor and out onto the balcony, offering her his jacket, and then leaning her over the balustrade for a passionate first kiss.

Nowhere was it ever written that the old letch had yellowing teeth and sour breath that reeked of bourbon, and leered at the young lady like he wanted to violate her in all sorts of ways, some quite possibly illegal.

Well, the leering part might have been in the movies I saw, but it was always reciprocated by the maiden. And it never felt this creepy.

I quickly looked around, getting my bearings. He'd steered me to what looked like a hallway that led to maybe the kitchen or somewhere, but was totally deserted. There were a couple of closed doors along the hall and then a larger door at the end. I hoped to see some of the kitchen staff bustling about, but it became obvious that whatever this hallway had been used for earlier, it was no longer in play.

"Sir, I think we should return to the reception. We can barely hear the music from here." My mind was playing for time. Maybe the old coot just had bad eyesight and didn't notice he'd wandered away, though the swinging door behind us should have been a good indicator.

"We can make our own music," he said. Seriously, he said that cheesy line. I couldn't believe it.

I was walking a fine line here. Obviously this guy was somebody important, or my dad wouldn't have nearly pissed his pants with glee to have me dance with him. But political bigwig or not, I wasn't going to get banged up against a hallway door with my bridesmaid's dress hiked around my waist.

At least not by this old perv. Now, if Montrose had been

my dance partner…

Edgar brought our clasped hands together, close to his chest. Which was fine, except it was apparently just an excuse for him to rub the back of his hand against my boob.

A shiver of revulsion spread through me, and I tried to disengage, put some space between us. But he only followed me, then took me further, pinning me up against the wall. For somebody his age, he was surprisingly strong.

All pretense of dancing had dropped, and he stared down at me with a look of contempt and desire. Still holding on to my hand, he now openly groped my boob, not even pretending it was a casual, mistaken brush.

"Mr. Prescott, please," I said, giving his shoulder a little push.

A creepy-ass smile crossed his face. "Yes, that's it. Beg me a little bit. I like that." His voice was cold, unfeeling, and that revulsion turned to dread.

"I'm only eighteen years old!" I didn't mention that I'd be turning nineteen very soon. Most likely that would only hurt my case.

"So, not jailbait. Jailbait. Jaybird. Sounds the same," he said, chuckling like he'd just cracked the best joke in the world. I wanted to crack his head.

"Jane. My name is Jane."

"I like Jaybird better," he said as his other wrinkled hand slid off my hip and down to my butt. "It suits you," he added as he squeezed. "God, you are one sexy girl."

"Emphasis on *girl*," I said, and he squeezed again.

Great, I get through this whole frickin' weekend and now I had to make a scene 'cause some dirty old man had a few too many cocktails.

"God, you have that same…whatever it is…that your mother had. No wonder Joe pissed it all away to get between her legs. I'll bet you're a real firecracker in bed."

This was bad.

I knew I could yell for help, and I would if it got that far. But that would bring people through the doors from the dance floor, and who knew who would find us. God forbid it'd be someone with a camera. Which was just about everybody with a phone.

I did not want to cause a scene, did not want any more attention on me than I'd already had today, but the old guy was strong and he was starting to push himself on me.

His hand mauled my boob, and I had realized I was just going to have to take my chances with the rest of the reception guests and call for help when Edgar removed himself from my body.

Or *was* removed, I realized, as I saw a flash of black tux, white shirt and hair lift Edgar off me and push him up against the opposing wall. The guy held Edgar there with a hand planted firmly and unrelentingly in the middle of Edgar's chest.

"You all right?" he said to me.

I nodded, unable to speak. Speechless upon seeing whom it was who'd saved me…at least from public humiliation, if not from Edgar himself.

"You?" I said, stunned to see my knight in shining armor.

SIX

❖

"**DO YOU HAVE** any idea who I am?" Edgar Prescott said.

"I couldn't give a flying fuck. But if I had to guess, I'd say you were some old goat who had too much power for too many years and thought he could get away with just about anything," Stick said.

Stick. Unbelievable that this was the guy who was helping me out. He hated me. And he—

"What are you even doing here?" I asked him. But skeevy old Edgar took that the wrong way.

"You see? The young lady wishes you to leave us alone," he said, and took a step back toward me.

Stick swiftly moved in front of me, facing Edgar. "I think you've got it wrong, Gramps. Tell him, Jane."

I was about to give Edgar Prescott a scorching—*blistering!*—set down when something inside me twitched.

"Mr. Prescott, Edgar. I really think it's best if you return to the reception. Someone of your stature can't be absent for long without people beginning to wonder why. And the last person you were dancing with was me. People will talk."

He waved this away, the movement making Stick's back stiffen, as if readying for an attack. I put my hand out, resting it on the small of Stick's back, silently telling him that I had this.

"I've been dealing with these people my whole career—

they will talk or not talk when I say so," Edgar said. The arrogance of this guy.

"Yes, of course," I said, placating the old fart. "But there were also several members of the press here tonight, and photographers."

That did it. I didn't know Edgar from Adam before tonight, but it was obvious by the look on his face that maybe the press did not ask "how high" when this guy said "jump."

I saw it the second that good sense—or maybe political self-preservation—prevailed and Edgar gave up on the idea of having Sweet Baby Jane up against the corridor wall.

He straightened himself up, adjusting his bow tie and running his hands through his thinning combed-over hair.

Just as he was taking a step back—again making Stick tense—Grayson Spaulding came through the same door that Edgar had propelled me through.

Sharp man—he took the scene in, and in seconds had come to the rightful conclusion. He gave me a questioning look—if I was all right. I nodded. He took in Stick standing in front of me. Then he placed a hand on Edgar's shoulder and said, "Edgar, the press would like to get a sound bite from you. Why don't you honor them with one of your trademark *bon mots*?"

Edgar was nodding as Grayson spoke, like he was coming up with the idea on his own. "If you'll all excuse me," he said with, like, this gentlemanly half-bow toward Stick and me. Like he hadn't just been pawing me and trying to squeeze my boob.

"Why you old—"

I pulled on Stick's tux jacket, cutting him off (and why was Stick in a tux?), then smoothed my hand on his back, making him stop before he pissed Edgar off and undid my and Grayson's smoothing of the situation.

He stopped what he was about to say, and even leaned

back a little, into my hand. I kept it there. The heat of him radiated through his shirt and the heavy tux jacket. He felt solid and safe beneath my hand. But I knew that Stick was anything but safe.

Edgar exited the corridor through a different door, which Grayson pointed him to, so that he'd reappear at the reception from a different direction than I would.

I didn't doubt for a moment that Grayson had this place totally wired for every side door entrance and exit. And honestly, I wasn't surprised that he'd come to find Edgar and me.

But Stick had gotten to me first.

"What are you doing here?" I said softly to his back, my hand still on him.

He started to turn to face me, but Grayson stepped toward us, causing Stick to stand at attention in front of me again.

Stick didn't know Grayson Spaulding. To him, Grayson could just be another political horndog come to take his turn with me.

It was kind of sweet, really. In a most fucked-up way.

"Stick. Grayson Spaulding," he said, holding his hand out for Stick to shake, which he did. Stick didn't step away from me, though, and I found I liked that. My hand, like it had a mind of its own, absently smoothed up and down his long back. I watched, almost hypnotized, as my pale hand brushed along the black tux.

"It's good to finally meet you in person," Grayson was saying to Stick after they shook hands. Stick only nodded in return.

And that broke the spell that had been woven over me. My hand dropped from Stick's back, and the loss of contact had him turning to me, but also facing Grayson, forming an odd little triangle.

"Jane, you're okay?" Grayson asked. Well, not exactly

asked. There was a question mark at the end of it, but his tone was one of…confirmation. Like he was congratulating himself for being right about me. That I could handle myself. As if letting me dance with that old letch had been okay.

Although it had been my father that had gleefully handed me over to Edgar Prescott. Grayson had taken a step toward us…to stop it?

"You knew he'd try something, didn't you?" There was some accusation in my voice, but like him, it was mostly about confirmation.

"Edgar has been known to…"

"Prey on the weak?"

Stick snorted. "Yeah, right. You're hardly what I'd call weak."

"To you. To Edgar I'm the daughter of a whore whose father would gladly pimp her out for the backing of a dirty old man."

"Now, Jane—" Grayson started, but I cut him off.

"You know that's true. Or mostly true. He handed me over to him without a moment's thought, and I'm willing to bet that good old Edgar's reputation for accosting girls is well-known in your circles."

Grayson didn't say anything. Stick was studying me, his brow furrowed.

"Anything could have happened to me if he hadn't shown up," I said, jabbing a thumb at Stick.

"Hardly," Stick said, obviously not liking the label of hero I was kind of throwing at him. Yeah, it didn't sit too well with me, either. "Another second and you would've had that perv on his knees, grabbing his gonads."

That was probably true. But then—

"But then Edgar would have had it out for Jane. This way, you're the one who interfered, Stick. And in Edgar's eyes, Jane was interrupted from something she wanted."

A chill went through me, an actual, physical chill.

"Christ, that's fucked up," Stick said, and Grayson nodded his agreement.

"Wait," I said. "You said 'meet in person,' like you'd already met in some other way?"

"Yes. Stick and I have been…conversing on the phone for a few weeks now. He's here tonight at my invitation."

The way Stick raised a brow at Grayson's explanation made me realize there was way more going on here than new phone buddies extending a wedding invite. Not that that, in and of itself, wouldn't be the most bizarre thing imaginable.

Then it hit me. "He's spying on Lily and Lucas for you." A weird look passed between them. "That's it, isn't it?" Again with the looks, and I knew I'd nailed it. "Dude, that's messed up," I said to Stick. "He's your best friend. He went to jail for you."

"You don't think I know that?" Stick said, taking a step closer to me. He was now closer to me, more on top of me than Edgar had been, but I felt none of the same feelings of fear and dread that I'd had then.

"Listen, here's what's going to happen," Grayson said with the authority that came from years of telling political powerhouses exactly what to do. "You two are going to go back out the door you danced through, Jane. You're going to dance your way out onto the floor. Like you've been dancing together this whole time. Closely. Like you want to be…dancing together. I want people wondering who Stick is to you, not where you were with Edgar for so long."

"Jesus," I whispered. Shit just got real.

"I know this has been a lot for you to deal with—this whole weekend. And especially finding out that your father is getting back into politics." He placed a hand on my shoulder.

Stick tensed, and I had this weird moment where I wanted

to reach out and hold Stick's hand. But of course I didn't, and the moment passed, thank God.

"And I know you don't want any of this, Jane. That you abhor this kind of life, the spotlight. You've worked very hard to distance yourself from it. But we don't always get to choose our destiny. Sometimes it chooses us."

"What a load of shit," Stick said. But Grayson was right in a way. Oh, all that lofty crap about destiny was just to stroke my ego, like he'd done to Edgar. But he was right about not having any choice.

I had deluded myself into thinking I could be someone else, somebody other than Jaybird.

But it looked like Jaybird was coming home to roost.

SEVEN

✦

"SO, JUST WHO the hell are you, Jane Winters?" Stick asked me while he held me in his arms and moved to the music.

Thankfully the band was playing a slow song as we made our way back onto the dance floor, and we were swallowed up by the very large crowd.

I'm a tall girl, but Stick was just the perfect height to dance with—I only had to raise my arm up a tiny bit to rest on his shoulder. His hand that held mine was cool and very rough. But strong. And it felt extremely good after having held that old buzzard's hand.

Maybe too good.

Because Stick was a car thief. And what's more, I was pretty sure he was kind of a head honcho. Lily's guy Lucas had been arrested while stealing a car for Stick.

Granted, Stick had offered to turn himself in to free Lucas, but thankfully it hadn't come to that and the charges against Lucas were dropped. Because of Grayson Spaulding's power and my acquiescence to be a bridesmaid at this wedding.

A pawn in my father's reintroduction to political life.

"Nobody," I said, answering Stick's question. "I'm nobody."

"Not likely," he said as he pulled me closer. It was to avoid a rather drunk couple that was veering toward us, but I noticed he didn't loosen his hold on me once the couple had danced—stumbled—past us.

And God, I would never admit it to him (and barely to myself), but it felt very nice to be held so closely by Stick.

I'd never seen him with less clothes than he was wearing now, but he had what seemed like a very hot bod. Or at least the kind that appealed to me. It wasn't as broad and muscular as Lucas, but tall and lean, almost rangy. And I could feel the strength of him in his grip on my hand, and throughout his back when I'd had my palm on it. And now, his shoulder under my hand…I could feel the muscles bunching as we would turn.

I could also feel the eyes upon us.

"Bullshit. Nobody." He gave a soft snort. His eyes darted around the dance floor and beyond. We'd moved through the throng a bit and were now more centrally located, where the press could see us.

And they did. Flashbulbs—which had been perpetually flashing—were now concentrated solely on Stick and me. It was like a lightning storm directed right at me.

"Shhh. Easy," Stick said, low and soft in my ear. He'd felt my body tense at the flashes.

His arm snaked around my waist, pulling me even closer. And damn, but my hand slid up and around his neck.

He typically wore his longish hair loose. About chin length, it was wavy and a light brown, but with some natural highlights that women would pay top dollar for in a salon. Tonight he had it slicked back and in a small club of a ponytail, which just brushed the collar of his tux. And now just brushed the back of my hand as I laid it at the back of his neck.

"Wanna give 'em a show?" he whispered in my ear, then placed a soft, chaste kiss on my forehead.

I looked up at him, and his eyes dropped to my lips, relaying his idea to me. I weighed the options in my head—

would it be prudent to have the press see me kiss a boy on the dance floor? A boy that wasn't crusty Edgar Prescott?

No. It would be just jumping from the frying pan to the fire. If I was going to be thrown into this world—and it looked like I hadn't really been given a choice—I was going to do it on my terms. Dictate as much as possible in a world where I had no power.

"Better not," I said, meeting his eye. And then—and I swear it wasn't my intention—my gaze dropped and I looked at his lips. He had a very nice mouth, with full lips. I didn't know that I'd ever seen Stick smile. And just as I was thinking that thought, his mouth lifted into a wide—and oh-so naughty—grin. I looked up to his eyes, and they were staring down at me. Mischief and…something else, something very raw, shining through.

"When have you ever done the smart thing, Jane Winters?" he said as he bent and kissed me.

The flashbulbs ratcheted up to double time, and I closed my eyes to block them out. And, okay, yes, to better feel Stick's kiss.

He tasted like champagne. And he smelled like fine wool and some expensive cologne. It was like kissing a rich Bribury boy. And Stick was most definitely not a Bribury boy.

Just as I was about to open my mouth to him, we were jostled by another couple. I opened my eyes, slightly dazed, and looked around.

The couple that moved me out of my kissing haze was Grayson Spaulding and his wife. He gave me a pointed look.

Yep, into the fire.

"You shouldn't have done that," I said to Stick. He seemed a little dazed, too. And there hadn't even been any tongue.

He took in the photographer frenzy and looked back to me. "No, probably not." Then that grin came back and he added, "Wanna do it again?"

I barked out an unexpected laugh. And realized how good it felt to laugh. It'd easily been since before I left for break that I'd had a good laugh.

Not a lot of chuckles around my mom these days as she seethed about the idea of the Stratton family wedding, of which she would not be a part.

And that it was Stick of all people who had delivered my first laugh in...days?...weeks?

That thought pissed me off. I didn't even like Stick. He was a car thief, for God's sake. He was responsible for Lucas being arrested, which in turn broke up him and Lily. At least for a while. I did not want Stick to be the one to make me laugh.

And certainly not the one whose kiss made me just a bit too tingly.

Putting my armor back in place, but keeping my smile on for the photographers, I said, "So, does Lucas know you're Grayson Spaulding's spy? That you're keeping an eye on him and Lily?"

Which still didn't explain what he was doing here tonight, with no Lucas or Lily in sight.

"Lucas is aware of my...employment with Spaulding."

That took me aback. Until... "Oh, you're both playing him? Take his money, but report back to him only what Lucas wants him to know?" I kind of appreciated that—it was a move worthy of Grayson Spaulding himself.

"No, Jane," he said, exasperation in his voice. The song ended, and couples filed off the dance floor, but Stick held me firmly in his arms and waited until the band struck up the next song, also a slow one.

He began moving me around the floor again as he said, "You're the one who jumped to the 'spying on Lucas and Lily' conclusion. You're way off base. Spaulding has accepted that Lily is dating Lucas. I don't think he's thrilled that his princess is dating a dropout townie…but he accepts it."

"So what are you doing for Grayson, then?"

He looked away from me, not meeting my eye. He pretended he was looking at the other dancers back out on the floor, but I think he was just avoiding my gaze.

Finally a shrug, and a sigh, then he looked back down at me. "I'm doing various special projects for him."

"Since when?"

"Since shortly after Lucas was arrested."

I shook my head, confused. "I'm not getting it."

Another shrug. "No reason why you need to. It doesn't concern you."

Well, now that just pissed me off. "And what special project needs to be done tonight? At my…Betsy's wedding?" He noticed the stumble in my words (it was still hard to call Betsy my sister) and seemed to be mentally filing it away. Damn him. I'd be wise not to underestimate Stick.

"Does somebody here need a car stolen for them? Is that why you're here? Call in a professional? There must be some primo cars in the lot tonight."

"Get in the barbs now, and make up better ones than that lame-ass one. 'Cause I am…extricating myself from my former profession."

"And does that *extrication* have a prison sentence attached to it?"

His mouth hitched up a smidge at the corner, like he was trying not to smile. And it made me try hard not to smile too. I did not want to share in private jokes with Stick.

"Just what the hell is your real name, anyway? Stick what? And what's your first name?"

He allowed the grin that time. Of course he had—he

knew he'd pissed me off. "It's just Stick."

"Like Cher? Yeah, you are kind of a diva."

"Like the Rock."

I snorted, and he twirled me in a bit of a dance move that made the skirt of my dress flare out in a soft swath of peach satin.

Much as I didn't want to be a bridesmaid, I did have to admit that the dresses Betsy picked out were pretty sick.

A fitted bodice, and then the flared skirt. Tea length, with an overskirt of cream lace. It was almost like the thing was designed with my tall, but curvy, frame in mind.

I loved how I looked in it, only wishing that I was wearing it to an event I wanted to attend.

Stick twirled me again, the dress flaring once more. And I felt…nearly beautiful.

I know I'm not. Lily is beautiful. Syd, our other roommate, is too, in a nontraditional way. But not me. I'm not bad looking, and seem to get my share of attention (even from those who don't know my backstory), but my mother says that comes from my "energy." I roll my eyes when she tells me this, but it doesn't mean that she's wrong.

"Killer dress, by the way," he said, as if he could read my mind. The song came to an end just as I spotted Montrose at a table with some of the other bridesmaids and groomsmen, presumably his friends from Brown. He was watching Stick and me dance with a serious expression on his face.

I broke from Stick and started walking that way, intending on asking Montrose to dance with me. The band was breaking and some old, jazzy big-band song came through the sound system, the DJ picking right up, allowing no lull.

Stick followed my eyes to Montrose's table, and grabbed my hand. "Come on, let's make that dress fly," he said as he pulled me back into the thick of the dancers.

Who knew Stick Whatever would be such a good dancer? He twirled me and led me, and we did indeed make my dress fly. It was almost…joyful the way my body moved with the music. At one point, dancers even moved out of the way to watch Stick twirl me around the floor.

I laughed and caught him smiling, and everything—even Edgar Prescott's hand on my boob—seemed a million miles away.

Until the music slowed and Stick pulled me back into his arms and I saw all the people sitting at tables along the dance floor edge. And was shocked to see Caroline Stratton and Grayson Spaulding sitting together, their heads close, talking. And looking straight at me.

"Oh, God. We probably shouldn't have done that," I said to Stick.

"What? The kiss? Or the kickass dancing?" There was a teasing in his voice and almost a lightness in his eyes when I looked up at him.

"Both. Grayson and Caroline are over there. And looks like they're talking about me."

He twirled me around so that he was looking at the tables. His eyes went right toward Caroline's table. She must have caught him looking, because Stick gave a nod of acknowledgement in her direction.

"I don't think they're discussing you," Stick said.

"I'm just surprised to see them together. From what I understand, they can't stand each other." It was kind of like they were both vying for my father back in the day, during the campaign. And from what I'd picked up over the years, it seemed like they blamed each other for my father succumbing to my mother's…charms. Grayson faulting Caroline for her being what he felt was cold. And Caroline felt Grayson should have been aware of my father's affair with my mother and nipped it in the bud. Or at least before my mother could get herself knocked up with me.

"Maybe they're just putting it all behind them to rally around your father. Kind of like you are."

"So you *do* know who I am?" I said, suspicion seeping through my voice.

"Who your father is? Yeah. How you came into being? Yep. I've got the background facts down." He slowed, pulling me back into his arms, making me gasp in a girly way that I hated. Sliding his hand along my waist, he guided me toward the edge of the floor. "But who *is* Jane Winters?" He slid his hand down and squeezed my ass. Before I could swat at his hand, he released me and smiled. "I don't have a fucking clue. Do you?"

He walked away, through the dancers, swallowed up by the tuxes and designer dresses.

EIGHT

JANUARY SUCKED.

I mean, I know January sucks everywhere, but it particularly sucked for me at Bribury.

And it wasn't even that we were having a bad winter. Comparatively it'd been pretty mild, hardly any snowfall at all, and when it did come it only stayed on the ground for a day or two before melting.

But Lily and Lucas were in love. And though I was happy for them, it also took my roommate away from the partying I wanted to do.

Oh, Lily tried not to be that girl. The one who dumps her friends for a new boyfriend. And Lucas worked nights, so during the week, Lily was free in the evenings.

But even when we did go to a party or something together, Lily wasn't interested in any of the guys there.

I wasn't quite ready yet to confess that I wasn't either.

I thought about Montrose. Even put myself in his path a few times. He was teaching a few sessions, but they were all of the one class that I'd taken last semester.

The couple of times I would accidentally on purpose run into him, he would be polite, but still call me Ms. Winters like he'd done in class. He never mentioned seeing me at Betsy's wedding.

The third time I saw him, he actually stopped and talked for a bit. He asked if I remembered what he'd said to me on my last day of his class.

I waved my mittened hand in the air and said, "Yeah, vaguely. Kind of how I should find myself and be true to her."

That wasn't exactly it. I, of course, knew every word he'd said. One: because he'd taken me aside, away from even Syd, who'd been asked to stay behind too, and I thought maybe my constant flirting was about to pay off. And two: because the words he said were ones I'd thought of nearly every day since.

"You're so busy not being who you are, perfecting the persona you've got going on, that you might not be able to find yourself when you need to. Find her. Be her…and let the rest of the bullshit go."

Yeah, I hated how he'd nailed me. And yet hadn't really at all.

He'd nodded that day in the quad and said he remembered every word, and that now he was thinking that maybe his advice to me had not been the best.

When I asked what he meant by that, he just looked off across campus, obviously in his own thoughts, and shook his head.

He said goodbye to me, and something in it felt…final. I didn't put myself purposely in his path after that.

I thought Syd might step up and fill the void left by Lily being in love. Syd liked to party, and she'd seemed desperate to be accepted by the Bribury boys.

But she'd picked up a second part-time job this semester, so I barely even saw her anymore. Even less than Lily.

Yes, I could have made more—other—friends. But I was kind of content to just hibernate through January myself. I liked the classes I was taking (though there was no hottie like Montrose teaching any of them), and though I'd never really needed to study, I did enjoy reading the textbooks.

One was *Intro to Psychology*. I'd been playing armchair shrink for years (with my parents, how could I not?) and found that most of my hypotheses actually had merit.

I thought once January passed I'd want to go out more, but coming home from my afternoon classes on a Tuesday in early February felt much the same as it had since coming back from break—stale.

The room was crisp, with a fresh breeze coming from the window that Lily had left open a tiny crack.

Which meant she and Lucas had had crazy monkey sex all afternoon before Lucas would have left to get his little brother from school.

Closing the window, I looked down to the frozen quad below me, watching my fellow Briburians (yes, just made that up…but I kind of like it) scurry to class, bodies huddled into their warm coats, knit beanies firmly placed on their heads.

I walked through our shared bathroom to Syd's room to see if she was around, but her room was empty.

I was just reaching for my phone to text Lily and see where she was when it beeped with a text tone that wasn't assigned to anyone, just the generic tone. I didn't get a lot of those. I liked knowing who was texting or calling, so gave specific tones to everyone.

That way I could ignore my father or mother without even having to reach for my phone to see it was them. Big timesaver.

Are you in your room? read the text.

Umm…yeah…like I was going to answer that.

It's Stick.

Oh. Okay, so it was at least someone I knew, if not someone I wanted to hear from.

Why? I answered.

Downstairs. Have something for you.

I knew he couldn't get into the dorm without a student ID, but this was Stick, and I wouldn't put it past him to worm his way in somehow. He knew what room we lived in because he'd come here the night Lucas was arrested.

And I didn't want him in the room with me right now. Not because I didn't trust him. And certainly not because I'd been replaying that kiss over and over in my mind since it had happened.

Because I hadn't.

Not too much, anyway.

What is it?

Can't say. You need to see it.

I'll be right down. I grabbed my jacket, still warm from my body. Phone and keys in hand, I took the stairs down. Made him wait a little.

I walked through the main entrance but didn't see him waiting against the pillar where Lucas was always waiting for Lily.

"Jane. Over here," he called, and I turned and walked around the large pillar looking out onto the circular drop-off area. There were six metered spots in front of the dorm, always taken. The one-way drive was wide enough for three cars, which was good because there was always at least one car next to every metered one with people being picked up or dropped off, or, like, pizza delivery guys. That left one lane for people to actually drive through. And sometimes that was taken up too.

Stick was standing in front of a black sports car, with his red car parked behind it. "Hurry up, will ya? I'm freezing my nuts off."

I walked toward him, surprised to see somebody behind the wheel of Stick's car. I ducked my head to look, thinking maybe it was Lucas, but it was just some guy about Stick's age that I didn't recognize. He nodded at me and I nodded back.

The engine was running.

I walked up to Stick and said, "What's going on? What do you have to give me?"

Okay, I knew I'd watched too many romcoms with my mom when I was younger when the first thing that popped into my head was Stick whispering, "This," and taking me into his arms and kissing me like he'd done on the dance floor.

Make no mistake, if he'd tried it I would have kneed him in the balls, like I should have done at the wedding.

"This," he said, and took my hand. His were bare, and my mittens were still in my dorm room. He dropped a set of keys into my palm then curled my fingers over to make a fist over them.

His hands were indeed freezing, and they hesitated for a moment on mine, like he was trying to warm them up on me or something.

"What are these to?" I asked, taking my hand from his and opening my fist. They were car keys, and the key chain was heavy silver with a Corvette insignia.

Stick took a step away from the black car he'd been standing in front of. Which was, of course, a Corvette.

"I don't get it," I said.

"It's yours," he said, like it made perfect sense.

"You stole me a car? I mean, I figured I was a good kisser, but come on—you didn't need to steal a car for me as a thank-you."

He snorted. "Please. You should be thanking me for that kiss. And I didn't steal the Vette."

"Oh, 'the Vette,' is it?" I took a step around him, to look more fully at the car. *My* car?

"So if you didn't steal it—"

"It's from your dad, okay?" There was definite tone in his voice. He did not appreciate the car thief joke. Which, of course, meant I'd have to save a bunch to use on him.

Though it wasn't like I was hoping to see him again or anything.

"This is from my dad? Are you sure?"

"Yep. Via Grayson Spaulding."

Ah, that made more sense. He'd texted me last week that he'd be in touch soon about doing that interview.

My dad had announced his candidacy shortly after the wedding. And, true to his word, Grayson Spaulding had somehow made Bribury a no-fly zone for reporters.

But soon I'd be asked to make an appearance and say how great my daddy was and how I thought he'd make a super governor of Maryland.

Apparently the Corvette was a sweetener.

"But why a Corvette?" I thought aloud. "Why not a cute little Audi, or a Porsche or something?"

"Had to be an American-made car, is what he told me."

Right. For appearances. I couldn't be driving a German or Japanese car up to campaign rallies, now could I?

"And you picked it out?"

Stick nodded, a rare flash of…pride? shining on his face.

"And *this* is what you thought I'd want to drive?" The flash of pleasure disappeared from his face, and for just a second I felt kind of shitty for making that happen. But then I remembered this was Stick—just some low-level car thief.

"Whatever. Trade it for something else. The dealer's information is in the glove box. It's registered for Lot H, you know where that is?"

I nodded. It was the freshman parking lot about a quarter of a mile from our dorm.

"Then my work here is done. Keep it. Don't keep it. Whatever. You can work that out with your father, or Spaulding, or whoever."

He started to walk to his car, opening the passenger door to get in.

"Wait," I said as I peeked into the Corvette.

"What?" he said, totally impatient.

I turned to face him. "I can't drive a stick shift."

A look of pure exasperation crossed his face. "Are you shitting me?"

"Ah, that would be a no, I'm not shitting you. I can't drive a stick. So why don't you go park it in Lot H for me and then bring me back the keys and I'll get Grayson on the phone to take care of it?"

He walked back to me, snatched the keys out of my hand. "That's how it's always been for you, hasn't it? Make a call and have someone else take care of it."

He wasn't really saying this to me, it was mumbled under his breath, and I suspected it was directed at everyone whom Stick perceived as a "have" to his "have not," but it still pissed me off.

"That's not at all how it's been for me. You may think you know all about me—and you might know more than most from your new BFF Grayson Spaulding—but you don't know *shit* about me." I took the keys back from him. "Go on, get out of here. I'll figure it out and get the damn thing to the parking lot myself."

"You can't just figure it out. You'll strip the gears, or kill—"

"I said I'd figure something out. I'm sure some guy on my floor can drive it there for me."

"And I just know how you'll repay him, too." He stepped closer to me, staring me down.

My eyes narrowed on his, but I managed a tiny, sexy smile. "Yes, I'll make sure it's worth his time…and effort," I said in a breathy voice that I wasn't even aware I had in my repertoire.

He placed a hand on my shoulder and slowly slid it down

my arm, brushing the back of my hand, then tightened his hold on my wrist and turned it upward. He took the keys back. "Do you have any more classes today?" he asked softly, still staring at me. I shook my head. "Anywhere you're supposed to be in the next few hours?" he asked. Another shake from me.

He sighed, then looked to the sky, raking a hand through his messy hair. No warm beanie for Mr. Hardass. "Christ," he whispered under his breath as he turned away from me.

He walked to his car and opened the passenger door. "I'll call you if I need you. Be available," he said to the guy behind the wheel, who nodded his understanding. He then reached into the front seat and grabbed a small white paper sack, which he shoved into his jacket pocket. Stick shut the door, and the red muscle car drove away.

Leaving me with Stick and my own muscle car.

"Let's go," he said as he opened the passenger door of the Corvette and waved me in.

"Where are we going?" I asked, but made my way to the car, lowering myself onto the smooth leather seat, which was warm under my butt.

"Driving lesson," Stick said, then closed my door and walked across to the driver's side.

NINE

❖

"IS THIS A CONVERTIBLE?" I asked when we'd cleared the town of Schoolport.

"Yes," he answered, the only word he'd spoken since he'd driven away from my dorm.

"But it's February."

He looked at me like I was an idiot. "It won't *always* be."

Well, yeah, that was true.

"And aren't Corvettes the cars that men buy during their mid-life crises? Isn't this basically a 'I still have a penis and know how to use it' car?"

"I don't know about a penis, but you sure have a set of balls on you, so does that count?"

I looked to the side window, not wanting Stick to see the small smile his comment produced. "No, it doesn't count."

"The Corvette is an American classic. It's about power, but with style and class."

"But certainly not understatement." Smile gone from my face, I once again was facing the front, able to see him from the corner of my eye if I wanted to. Not that I did.

"Yeah, and you're such a master of understatement."

The corner of my mouth quirked up again, but I let that smile slide.

"Well I'm not all about style and class either. Or power,

for that matter."

"You don't think whatever you did to get Spaulding to take the leash off Lily took power?"

I shrugged. "I had something he wanted."

"Isn't that what power basically is?"

"Now you sound like one of them."

I saw his hand tighten on the gear shift next to me. "I am nothing like them."

I looked over at him, waited until he sensed it and took his eyes from the road to meet my eyes. "Neither am I," I said calmly but firmly.

He nodded, went back to not crashing my new car, and said, "Fair enough."

We were driving through downtown Chesney now. I hadn't been back through since the wedding. We passed the Marriott and neither of us said a word. I wondered if he was thinking about dancing with me. Or…the other part of that.

A turn later and we drove past the club that Stick had dragged me out of months ago when Lily had been worried about me.

"Bang that prof yet?" he asked, speaking of Montrose, who I'd been trying to snag when Stick took my hand and literally pulled me out of the club.

"What's it to you if I have or haven't?"

He shrugged, and downshifted (is that what it was called? That was why I was on this lesson, I suppose). "Nothin' to me." He put the car in neutral as we came to a red light. He looked over at me. "And I'm guessing it'd be nothing to you, either."

"What's that supposed to mean?"

His eyes were brown and held a glint of…was that *judgment*? "Nothing," he said, turning away from me and revving the engine.

Okay, the low, deep—and yes, powerful—engine-revving

of a Corvette was kind of cool. Not that I would admit that to Stick.

"No, really. What did you mean by that?" My tone was not one of confrontation, but more of friendly curiosity, though I felt differently inside.

"I'm guessing he'd just be another notch on your bedpost. An important notch, because of him being a prof and, you know, you were the pursuer."

My face began to burn, but I wasn't the type to blush. Too much had happened to me when I was a kid to have any blush ability left by now.

"How do you know I wasn't the pursuer with all the guys I've slept with?"

We'd cleared the Chesney city limits and were now entering the neighboring countryside. Having bare, open road in front of us, Stick quickly picked up speed, the vista racing by. A part of me really responded to this—the feeling of speed and power in this car—as we sped away from everything.

"I don't know, but I'm guessing you weren't. Oh sure, the important ones, like a prof, or, I don't know, the fucking prom king or whatever. Sure, they were worth dogging after. But you let the others do the work the rest of the time." He glanced over at me; his face was blank and I couldn't read it—which pissed me off. "Am I right?" he asked with genuine curiosity in his voice.

"Are you slut-shaming me?" I asked, not really sure.

"Hell no. I'm all for slutty behavior. Bring it on, I say."

I snorted. "I'm sure you do. There are male sluts, too, you know."

"I *do* know. As there should be. Equal opportunity slutting. I'm all for it."

I couldn't hold back the smile that time, or even hide it. And damn if a little laugh didn't sneak out too.

He returned my smile, the engine roaring around us, and I thought of how his shoulders and arms had felt under the expensive wool of the tux he'd worn to Betsy's wedding. How warm the back of his neck had been, bared because of his short ponytail.

Today he wore his hair as I'd always seen it—loose and completely unkempt. Scraggly, even. But the waves were natural and untamed, and the rare February sunshine was picking up all the auburn-y highlights in the brown mass.

"So here we are," I said. "Just a couple of sluts driving through the Chesney countryside."

"I never called you a slut, Jane," he said softly.

He hadn't, I knew that.

"I just wanted to know if you slept with that guy. Just that one guy."

I don't know why I felt compelled to even answer him, let alone with the truth. "No," I said. "I didn't sleep with him."

"Is there a 'yet' at the end of that sentence?"

"No," I said softly, perhaps admitting it to myself as much as to Stick. I saw him make a small nod, almost to himself. "Why do you care, anyway?" I asked, but I knew. I knew it with the sick knowledge that you got when you were about to do something you shouldn't…but did it anyway.

"No reason," he said. But I heard in his voice that he knew too.

We drove for another ten minutes, taking a couple of turns that took us deeper into the countryside, but still on nicely maintained roads. I knew Stick wouldn't take my new car on any rutted dirt roads…he had too much respect for it.

Which I kind of liked. And I kind of respected him for it.

There were some gorgeous, mansion-type homes set deeply back from the road, with long, winding drives and gates at the front. But not many, and they were miles apart from each other.

"I'm assuming you've been watching, right? Are you ready to try it yourself?" Stick asked, slowing the Vette down and pulling to the side of the road. "There's no traffic on this road, and yet it's in good shape, so it's a great place to practice. There are some hills coming up, and you'll want to try those, downshifting and everything."

It sounded like a lot, but I nodded that I was ready to drive my own car, and reached to unbuckle my seatbelt.

"Atta girl," Stick said, seemingly genuinely pleased with me.

Which, I was pissed at myself to admit, made me pleased too.

I looked around. Something about the area seemed so familiar to me. "I think I've been here before."

"Oh yeah? Lately?"

I shook my head as Stick cut the engine and undid his own seatbelt. "No. Not lately. Maybe never. It's just I—"

"What?"

My head shook, more strongly now. "Nothing," I lied. I remembered now, and wished I hadn't.

I got out of the car, liking how I had to pull myself up and out of the snug, perfectly ass-fitting seat. Almost lamenting leaving it, even for the short time to get to the driver's side. I walked in front of the car, my hand gliding across the metal, which was both cold from the February air, and warm from the powerful engine underneath. I liked the pale of my hand against the deep black paint. Hmmm, maybe I would get black nail polish.

Stick stepped out of the car and held the door open for me. I slid in to the seat he'd just vacated, still warm from his body.

"You'll want to…good," he said as I found the seat adjuster

myself and brought the seat forward. I was tall, but Stick was taller, both of us having long legs.

"Is that why you're called Stick? Because you were as skinny as a stick when you were a kid?"

He rolled his eyes at me and closed the door, careful not to slam it. I knew my baby was in good hands with Stick, that he would treat her with kid gloves.

Oh, so now the Vette was my baby? And a she?

Stick got in the passenger seat and made a big show of snuggling into the seat. "I always said you had a smoking ass," he said in reference to the seat being warmed for him.

"My old man couldn't have splurged for seat warmers? In February?"

"Actually, she does have seat warmers. I was just pissed at you when we left Bribury so I thought I'd let you warm yourself up." He rocked in the seat. "Which you did very well."

Apparently Stick thought of my car as a "she" also. "Wait. What? Why were *you* pissed at *me*?"

He leaned over, stretching his arm to the back of my seat, just above my head. His face was very close to mine. "Because. Here you are given this amazing car…a gift. And all you can do is bitch about the type of car it is."

"Just to be clear, this car is not a gift. It is a bribe, or more accurately, an opening offer."

"To what?"

"More negotiations."

"Again…to what? Or *for* what?"

I shook my head. "Nothing. It doesn't matter." Not wanting to get into it with him, and still not fully understanding what role he was playing that he'd be at my sister's wedding and delivering me my new car, I changed the subject to something I knew would absorb him.

"So, seven-speed. What exactly does that mean?"

It worked. He spent the next twenty minutes explaining it all to me. He could tell I was itching to drive her ("her" slowly becoming "Yvette" in my mind), and finally waved for me to start her up. I put it in neutral like he'd explained and then turned the ignition.

The roar of her coming to life was powerful, and I placed both hands on the wheel to feel her vibrations run through me.

Stick smiled at my movements. "She's something, isn't she?"

In an odd way, I didn't trust my voice to answer him, so I just nodded.

"Okay. So we talked about the mechanics of it, but you can't really pick up the rhythm of her until you drive her yourself. And every car is different with their...needs."

I looked over at him, raising a brow. "Needs? Really?"

"Definitely. What this baby—"

"Yvette."

"What?"

"Her name is Yvette."

He studied me for a second, and then that grin, the one he'd had at the wedding just before he'd kissed me, came over his stern face. "God damn, but you might be a car person yet," he said, clearly pleased.

"Hardly."

But the grin stayed on. "Not very original," he said.

I shrugged. "She's my first car. What do I know about naming cars?"

"You're right. You'll learn."

I smiled at that, at him. His eyes dropped to my mouth, and suddenly the car got very small. "Right," he said, breaking eye contact and looking down at my feet. "So, yeah, finding the rhythm Yvette needs. Be gentle with her at first, but firm—she needs to know you're the boss."

"Oh Jesus, what are you, the Corvette Whisperer?"

"Why yes, yes I am." He motioned for me to get moving, and I did as he'd instructed me, easing my foot off the clutch while applying the gas and also putting it into first gear.

And we lurched forward and then conked out.

"Again," I said, before he could say a word. He just nodded as I went through the motions again, to the same result.

I expected him to jump in with some car-expert talk, or even just some guy-like tell-me-what-I'm-doing-wrong speak, but he stayed silent.

I almost liked Stick in that moment. Almost.

The third time, I got Yvette on the road in first, and drove at that speed for what felt like way too long.

"Listen to her," Stick said softly. He was very close to me, and I could feel his breath on my cheek. "She'll tell you when you need to shift. You'll feel it."

And I did. The movement wasn't fluid, but it wasn't as jerky as it had been, and I got her into second, increasing my speed.

"Yes, that's it." He moved his arm across the back of my seat and scooted a bit closer, leaning into the console. He rested a hand on top of mine, wrapped around the gearshift head.

"It's like sex. Or good sex, anyway. Listening to her, feeling when she's ready for more. Being gentle when you make your move, but also being sure."

He squeezed my hand as I eased my foot onto the clutch and shifted to third. "Exactly," he whispered.

The country road where we were driving was completely deserted and mostly straight, yet I didn't dare take my eyes from the road. And not because I was scared to crash.

I was scared to see the look I knew Stick was giving me.

I could feel my pulse picking up, and my heart racing in time with Yvette's. And I totally got what Stick was saying, totally felt her, felt Yvette.

The shift to fourth was seamless, and we sped down the country road, and I desperately wished that it was warm enough to put the top down. The next shifts also went well.

"Sixth? Seventh?" I asked Stick, not entirely sure what my baby needed. First-time mother, and all.

"Not yet. Let her get used to this first. It really is like sex. The early gears are foreplay. In fourth and fifth gear you're trying to maintain, to make it last, make it build. Sixth and seventh, she…you know."

His hand left mine and moved to my knee. I could feel the heat of him through my jeans. His big hand covered my knee, his fingers dangling down between my legs. His other hand moved from the back of the seat to my neck, gently resting beneath my hair. He moved aside the collar of the great peacoat I'd found at a navy surplus store, and put his fingers around the back of my neck.

His thumb began to slowly stroke my sensitive skin.

And I couldn't wait to go further.

TEN

✦

I STARTED TO DOWNSHIFT as I climbed a hill. A familiar hill. Stick gently squeezed my thigh, noticing my tension. "You're doing great. You've got her." He mistook my stiffening for my first big hill in Yvette. He didn't know what I knew.

Just over the hill, I saw it. The gates to a large estate, the last one on this road.

The Holy Grail if you were my mother, Pandora Winters.

Easing my way down the hill (I just wanted to put it in neutral and coast, but Stick said no), I decided to pull over. Just a bit before the gate, like we'd done so many times before.

"Um…want me to drive?" Stick asked. His hand had stilled on my thigh. Part of me desperately wanted that hand to keep climbing, to tease and tempt, to pull me out of the place that being in front of this estate took me.

"I just… Can we stop for a second?" I said.

"Sure," he said. Not a speck of sarcasm or derision from him. Weird.

I thought about turning to him, reaching for him, tasting him. But it was Stick, and it would have just been avoidance, so I didn't.

It was some sort of sick pull that had me reaching for the door. The air was cool and brisk, the wind whipped somewhat, and I raised my face to it, like I was daring it to give me its worst. And as if Mother Nature knew me well, the wind died suddenly, leaving my view of the house beyond the gates, just at the top of a tasteful rise, clear and unobstructed by gusting, bare tree branches.

In the spring and summer, you couldn't even see the house, the foliage was so thick, the tree line acting as a larger secondary gate.

I knew this because our pilgrimages were at various times and seasons. Pandora's whims were not on any kind of calendar that I could ever figure out.

And I'd tried. Relentlessly, desperately, until I'd gone to boarding school hours away. Though I wasn't entirely out of her line of fire there, at least I wasn't woken out of a deep sleep to go "for a ride…for ice cream," which would inevitably end up here, with her standing in front of the car, as I was now.

I moved around the front, my bare hand feeling the warmth of Yvette through the hood. She felt good, comforting.

I came to the passenger side, which was in front of the gate. Stick exited from the car but didn't say anything.

Until I started to lean against Yvette. "Hey, hey. Hold on," he said, pulling me by the waist and spinning me around. He did some kind of odd frisking thing, lifting up my peacoat and checking out my ass.

"Hey," I said, pulling away from him.

"Just checking for anything that will scratch the car," he explained, a bit too much humorous glint in his eyes for me to totally believe him. I gave him an "oh, please" look, and he said, "Seriously. You know what all those sparkly things on girls' jeans do to good cars?"

"I don't have sparkly shit on my ass."

"So I see, but I had to be sure."

I shrugged. "Why? You delivered her in pristine condition. Anything that happens to her now is on me."

A sickening look crossed his face. Seriously. Like he was literally going to be physically ill.

"You'll take care of her, right? I mean, I know shit happens, especially in winter, but, like, you're not going to just…" He waved his arms in an abstract way, apparently unable to articulate the possible atrocities I might perpetrate against my new car.

"Relax. I'll take good care of her. Like I've told you— many times—I'm not a silver spoon. I know the value of stuff." He looked at me skeptically. I reached out and put my hand on his upper arm, still warm from being in the car. "I'm serious. I won't be a douche to Yvette."

This eased him, and he nodded at me. We turned, standing side by side, both leaning against the side of the car.

I don't know if it was Stick showing me how to drive Yvette, or his genuine caring about her welfare, or just a moment of weakness on my part, but as I looked up at the gates I said in almost a whisper, "This is Caroline Stratton's house. My father's ex-wife."

"I know who she is," he said.

That's right. If he was working for Grayson Spaulding and had done enough digging to know about my background, he'd have heard about Caroline.

But he couldn't have known… "My mom and I used to drive out here and park right in this same spot."

"When?"

I shrugged, looking forward, not wanting to meet his eyes. I could feel him looking at me, and as if he knew I couldn't answer while he did, he turned and looked toward the house.

"A few times a year. I don't know how often she did it when I was a baby. Or if she even did, though I suspect so."

"Did you live close by?"

I shook my head. "Not close enough that it was a quick

drive over. We lived on the other side of Baltimore."

"And you'd just stand here? Like this?"

I nodded, though he wasn't looking at me. I think he *felt* it, though.

"Yeah. Sometimes she'd spew some bullshit about how it should be her and me living in that house. Most times she'd just look at it."

"And what would you do?"

I shrugged. "Nothing. At first I didn't understand why we *couldn't* live there, if she said we were supposed to be.

"And don't get me wrong, our house was no shithole. It was fine, perfect for just the two of us, really. My father supported me, just not…"

"In the style your mother thought you deserved."

"She saw Betsy and Joey being raised in this house and she said I should be raised in something just as big."

He waited for me to go on. "But at some point I realized it had nothing to do with me. It never did. For either of them. I was a tool my mother used, and a burden my father reluctantly bore."

Jesus, here I was giving my hard-luck story to a townie who was forced to steal cars for a living. Well, maybe forced, maybe gleefully willing. Either way…

"Sorry. I usually don't throw pity parties," I said, embarrassed. I sneaked a peek at him out of the corner of my eye. He shrugged, still looking up at the house.

"I don't know you real well, Jane, but you're right, you don't play the pity card. And you could. Definitely."

I lifted a hand and dropped it. "Well, everybody's got their shit, right?"

"Yeah, to a degree. But yours is knee deep and very public."

"Not anymore. I put my foot down. Changed my name, went to boarding school. Tried to distance myself from the crazy."

He was nodding. "That's good. It seems to have worked for you. And that's the one thing I noticed about you right from the start—or at least after I learned who you were."

"What?"

"That you never played the pity card, and you never *ever* played the 'do you know who I am' card."

"Why would I play that card? I didn't want anyone to know who I was."

"Exactly. Not everybody in your position would want that. They'd play it to the hilt. Want to be on a fucking reality show or something."

"God," I said, the thought literally sending a shiver through me.

Stick lifted an arm, like he was going to put it around me, but then dropped it. Must have remembered that he intensely disliked me.

And then I remembered why I'd received Yvette—for services soon to be rendered.

"But it's about to become that—a reality show."

"Yeah, I guess it is. But you have something they want—your public opinion of your father."

"I know, that's why the car."

"Yeah, I figured."

"Do you think I'm an asshole for taking it?"

He did turn to me then. Put his hands on my crossed arms and gave me a tiny shake.

"Are you kidding? They'll chew you up and spit you out and not think twice about doing it. The press, the political party, the campaign—Christ, even your own parents. I say take what you can when you can. Hold out for what you want and try to navigate the waters so that you're calling as many shots as you can."

"There won't be many I can call."

His hands softened on me, but he still hung on. And damn, but I was grateful that he did.

"I know. But play it like a chess game—look three moves ahead, know what pieces are the most valuable to them and protect your assets."

"You play chess?" I asked, with maybe too much incredulity in my voice.

His hands dropped away, and I was sorry I'd said it. "Nah, more of a checkers man, myself."

He grinned, but I knew I'd hurt him. Man, when I try it doesn't work, and when I don't want to…bullseye.

We sat in silence, just looking ahead, both lost in our own thoughts. Or maybe he was lost in mine, because when he finally spoke, he said, "So, like, would your mom ring the gate bell or anything? Leave a flaming bag of dog shit and run?"

I smiled, imagining Pandora running back to the car in her spiky heels after depositing a bag of poo.

"No, she'd just stare at the house. Sometimes mumbling, sometimes not."

"And your sister and brother were raised here?"

I nodded. "Yeah, it was the house they lived in when Joe and Caroline split up, so she stayed with the kids. I think she was looking for stability in Joey's and Betsy's lives. Even though she had lots of other choices."

"Yeah?"

"She came from money. Old, political money. That's why she and my father made such a great team—were considered the perfect match." I let out a small snort that perfectly conveyed my opinion of that vision. "The house on the cape where she and the kids summered was a family home. And there are more. When her parents died, she inherited a boatload of money and properties, but she always stayed in this home. The one that she lived in with my father."

"I'll bet that pissed your mother off even more."

I looked at him. "You catch on quick, son," I said. He gave me a tip of an imaginary cap. The wind kicked up just then and his hair blew against his face. Without thinking, I reached over and pushed it away, back, even as the wind blew mine across my eyes, temporarily blinding me.

Which was just as well. I didn't want to see what expression Stick had on his face with my fingers in his wavy hair.

"So, how long since you were last here?" he asked. His head moved into my touch, and I kept my hand there for a moment before removing it, ostensibly to brush the hair from my own face.

"Oh, let's see. I was maybe eleven or twelve. It took me a second today to remember this was the way to her house."

"And yet you kept driving this way," he said, pointing out that which I would have left untouched.

"Yeah. Playing the masochist card?"

He laughed, and God it sounded good amongst all these ghosts.

"Careful—that will lead to the pity card, and before you know it you'll have a whole damn deck."

I smiled. "You're right. Let's go. Enough of this maudlin bullshit. I love Bribury, I've got great friends and now I have Yvette. Yes, there will be a bunch of bullshit coming up with the campaign, but right now, right here, life is good."

He moved to face me, his back to the Stratton estate, blocking it from my vision. He stepped into me, his jeans brushing mine, his hoodie touching my coat. Lifting a hand, he brushed a finger across my cheek, then tucked a strand of hair behind my ear.

"Yeah, about that. I'm sorry, but I think I'm about to fuck with your 'all is right, right now' vibe."

"What do you mean?" Was it because he was going to kiss me? And would that mess with my vibe? Or make it better?

"I'll be right back. Wait here," he said, then turned and walked up to the gate. He reached for the gate panel.

"Come on, Stick, don't be an asshat," I said, assuming he was going to ring the bell, something even my mother never did.

He turned to me. "I have to drop something off. I'm…I'm sorry," he said, pulling the white paper bag out of the front pocket of his hoodie. Then, instead of ringing the intercom bell on the panel, he punched in a code and the damn gate started opening.

"Stick? What the hell?" I said, but he was already jogging up the long, winding drive, the gates slowly closing behind him.

I was in shock. Then pissed, though I wasn't certain why.

Screw this. I moved back around the car and settled myself into the cockpit, only to discover that Stick must have taken the keys from the ignition after I'd gotten out.

And still had them as he entered the home of Caroline Stratton.

ELEVEN

I STARED STRAIGHT ahead as Stick got back in the car fifteen minutes later.

"You don't want to keep driving?" he asked as he got into the driver's side. I had moved to the passenger seat while he'd been—still unfuckingbelievable!—in with Caroline Stratton.

"Nope," I said. "Let's go. I have a party to get to tonight."

"Montrose going to be there?"

No. There was no party. And since when did he know Montrose's name? "Yes, that's why I'm going."

It was probably the fast answer, or the pissiness of my voice, but Stick just snorted and said, "Yeah, right. Party my ass."

"Just drive, dickwad."

He roared Yvette to life, and I hated to admit that she seemed to like his touch better than mine. For now.

"Listen, I'm sorry. I should have said something sooner. Way before you talked about coming here as a kid."

"Umm…*yeah*, you should have."

"I didn't know that, though—that you used to come here with your mom. I thought you just randomly stopped at the bottom of the hill. I was going to explain whose house it was and why we were driving out here."

"So how about explaining it now?"

"Caro said to say hello, by the way."

"Caro? Jesus. What, am I, like, in bizarro world or something? What the hell is going on?" There wasn't whininess in my voice, it was something else, but I didn't like how it sounded.

Shape up, Jane. Don't let him see how this rattled you.

Never mind that it was Stick and I couldn't give a flying crap what he thought of me.

"I'm restoring her father's car collection."

"Her what?"

"Her father had a really extensive car collection. Which I guess is hers now. I guess he died a couple of years ago? And the mom a while before that?"

"Yes, she was their only child, and sole heir."

He chuckled. "Sole heir. I love how rich people talk."

I opened my mouth, ready for combat, but he held up a hand. "I know, I know, you're not rich. I get it."

"So, there are cars involved?" I said, wanting to get back to the matter at hand, crazy as it was.

"Yeah, twenty-two to be exact. And we're bringing them down from the dead guy's house in Boston. I guess she's selling that place or something."

I hadn't known that, but really, why would I? I had a sneaking suspicion that my mother did, though. She always seemed to be up on all things Caroline Stratton. Or Betsy or Joey.

I could attest to the fact that she'd grilled me for the rest of my holiday break once I got back from the wedding weekend. Every friggin' detail, asking me to describe all the people, what they were wearing, everything that was said.

I left out the crude comments about her that spewed from Edgar Prescott. Not because I wanted to spare her feelings, but more because I thought she'd take it as some weird-ass compliment that he remembered who she was.

"And some of these cars have been pretty neglected over the years. Still in great shape, just not the pristine condition that apparently her dad used to keep them in."

"And *you're* the one restoring them?"

"Yep."

We were out of the area with the gorgeous estates and heading back toward Chesney. Crazy, I know, but my breathing became more normal, my heartbeat slowed down. Just like it had when I was a kid and we'd be driving away. Relief would flood through me that nobody had seen us—caught us.

"What? There's nobody in Boston that can restore cars? That's a little hard to swallow."

"You have problems swallowing, Jane? I can help you out with that. It's all in releasing the back of your throat. I can teach you all about loosening up your gag reflex."

"Screw you," I said.

"Well, yeah, there's always that too. We could skip right to it."

I was about to throw another verbal volley when I realized that was what he wanted.

"Keep dreaming, asshole. Now, back to the cars. Isn't it kind of like handing the key to the henhouse over to the fox?"

"I told you, I'm done with that." There was a forcefulness in his voice, and it was deeper and a bit growly.

I believed him. For no reason really other than I just... did. But that didn't mean I couldn't continue to bust his balls about it. "Yeah, we'll see. I suppose it would be pretty stupid to steal what you've been entrusted with. And you may be a thief, Stick, but you ain't stupid."

"And I'm no longer a thief. So I guess that makes me a smart, stand-up guy."

"I didn't say smart. Just not stupid. There's a difference."

"Never give an inch, do ya?"

"Give an inch, they'll take a mile."

"Christ, and I thought *I* was guarded."

It shouldn't have made me bristle, but it did. Still, he wasn't wrong, so I decided to just let that one slide.

"So, back to the cars," I said.

We were driving through Chesney now, and I watched Stick's handling of Yvette at the stop lights, trying to store it in my memory.

"Yeah, you're going to need to practice with lights. And the first couple of times you'll probably stall out and the assholes behind you will honk their horns and start yelling. And that will tense you up and make you stall out again. Block 'em out and just listen to Yvette. She's the only one whose opinion matters when you're behind the wheel."

I was grateful for his words, because no doubt a bunch of people honking and yelling at me would tense me up. And then no doubt that I'd strike back, flipping them the bird and starting a nice little road-rage incident.

As we eased through the last light in town and hit open road toward Schoolport, Stick opened Yvette up and let her run. I again wished it was warm enough to put the top down.

"You'll be a master at driving her by the time it warms up enough to have the top down," Stick said, eerily reading my mind. "And then, man, will you be a sight on this highway. And down the freeway? To DC? Shit, they won't know what hit them." It wasn't like he was even talking to me. And perhaps he wasn't. He might have been talking to Yvette, because there was just a bit too much admiration in his voice for it to be directed at me.

The feel of her beneath us, so strong, so powerful— exactly the way I pretended to be and wished that I truly was. I admired her too, and was quickly becoming quite attached to my new baby.

"And so you're restoring these cars. Driving them down from Boston and—"

"Not driving them down. They're being brought down on semis. We don't want them on the road."

"Okay. So you're bringing them down from Boston and working on them here."

"Right."

"Forget for a minute that there must be three hundred guys in Boston that could be doing it."

He snorted. "Hardly. But yeah, it could be done in Boston. But she needed them off the estate there because of selling it, there's room for them here and I can do the restoration basically twenty-four seven, so she can put the whole collection on the market."

"She's selling her father's car collection too?"

He shrugged. "I think with Betsy married now, and Joey in Africa, she's doing some downsizing." He laughed. "Jesus, can you imagine a life where your downsizing is getting rid of a Boston estate, a car collection, and who knows what else, but keeping a place like the Chesney Hills house and a place on Cape Cod?"

"No," I said, "I can't imagine a life like that."

He looked over at me. "Sorry, I wasn't thinking."

I waved his apology away. "Believe it or not, I don't lament the fact that Betsy and Joey lived in a house like that—or several of them. It's not the money that I envied, it was—" I stopped, realizing what I was revealing—that I envied their situation in any way. And to Stick of all people, who would no doubt needle me about it and use it to his advantage.

But he didn't. He said nothing for the next fifteen minutes until we reached the town of Schoolport. Bribury was on the edge of town closest to Chesney. I happened to know that Stick and Lucas were from the other side of town. Literally from the wrong side of the tracks.

"Yeah, I know it wasn't—isn't—about the money for you, Jane. But a shitty home life is a little easier to take when you have your own wing of the house to hide out in."

"True," I conceded, though I would never know for sure. Still, it would have been nice to hide from Pandora and her periodic smothering.

But it did make me think about Stick's home life. "You sound like maybe you could've used that private wing growing up, yourself."

He shrugged, downshifting to take the corner onto the Bribury campus. "We've all got our shit to deal with. Joey Stratton is in Africa to escape his. So, yeah, maybe having a whole wing to hide in isn't even enough."

"And how'd you deal with your shit?"

He lovingly stroked Yvette's steering wheel and I had a flash of his long, strong fingers stroking me that way. "Cars," he said. "They were my salvation."

"And your income."

"That came later. I started working on cars when I was eight years old. Would just hang out at my old man's shop, handing him tools and shit. Nudie calendar on the wall, the smell of oil, allowed to get as dirty as I wanted—I thought it was the greatest place in the world."

"So why aren't you still working there? Instead of… restoring cars?"

He tensed, his knuckles whitening on the gearshift. It was so close to my knee, I almost wanted to touch it, but I didn't.

"Shop's gone. Father's dead."

"Oh, I'm sor—"

"Open the glove box. There's a sticker in there for Lot H."

He was obviously changing the subject. And as someone

who often did the same when the subject of parents came up, I gave him a pass.

I pulled out the sticker, peeled the back off and stuck it on the inside of the windshield in my corner. I might have imagined it, but I thought Stick winced. I kind of felt the same way—I didn't want any blemishes on Yvette.

"And don't go putting stupid-ass bumper stickers all over her, either," he said, thinking along the same lines as I was.

"I won't," I said, but not because he was telling me not to.

"She's too gorgeous to be a billboard for your political or social commentary."

"I won't. Jesus," I said under my breath, but loud enough for him to hear.

"Not even a 'Stratton for Governor' one."

"Right. As if."

We both smiled at the thought of that—me riding around town with a Joe Stratton sticker on my car. No way, no how. Though I supposed I was going to have to wear a button or something at campaign events this summer.

Another point to negotiate with Grayson Spaulding when the time came.

"How'd you get this sticker, anyway?"

"I registered the car for you with the admin office, got the sticker, got it all squared away."

"Thank you," I said, though I was pretty sure he'd done it all to protect Yvette, not me.

"I also installed an extra theft-protection system. If someone tampers with her locks, you'll automatically get a text. So will I."

"Okay." Wow, he'd gone to some trouble. This must be the kind of stuff he was doing for Grayson Spaulding—restoring Caroline's cars, getting one all set up for me. Still, it seemed like an odd coupling—Stick and Grayson. Throwing serene, refined Caroline into the mix even made it weirder.

"At first I hated the idea of you leaving her out here in a student lot. Still do, actually." We passed my dorm and took a right turn to head toward the edge of the small campus and the lots where students parked their cars.

Some colleges didn't even allow freshmen to have cars on campus, or only if you lived so many hundreds of miles away and got, like, a special dispensation or something.

But Bribury kids would not be denied their sports cars and luxury SUVs, and so all students were allowed to have cars on campus, but you had to walk quite a ways to get to them.

"But then I figured, what the hell—every car in this lot is going to be expensive as hell. I still think you should park her in a corner or something so someone is less likely to scratch or ding her."

"They tell women not to park in dark corners, or out by ourselves."

He nodded. "Yeah, that makes sense. I guess scratch that idea."

We entered Lot H and found a spot that was away from all the other cars, but still out in the open and under a light pole.

"Do you want me to drop you back at your dorm?" he asked as he pulled a phone out of his jeans pocket.

It was still light out, and I thought the walk would feel... refreshing after being so close to Stick for so long. "No, I want to walk."

He nodded, then flipped the phone open and dialed. "Yeah. Hey. I need you to pick me up at Lot H on campus." He listened, then said, "Now. Yeah. Thanks." He snapped the phone shut and put it back into his jeans.

"A flip phone? Seriously? Must not have been too good of a car thief if that's all you can afford. No wonder you're getting out of the business."

Out of his other pocket he pulled an iPhone, flashed it at me, then put it back. "I just haven't taken the time to transfer my numbers over yet."

"Because you just got the iPhone?" I wondered if Grayson Spaulding had gotten it for him. If I'd be expected to be in such close contact like that?

"No, I've had the iPhone for a couple of years."

Then I remembered watching *Sons of Anarchy* and that they all used flip phones that they could easily ditch and weren't traced to them in any way like a cell contract. "Burners," I think they called them.

"Oh," I said, getting it.

"Yeah, well, I'm using the iPhone mostly now, but still have some numbers that I haven't—or don't want to—transfer over."

"Your hoodlum buddies don't rate being in the iPhone contacts?"

He cut the engine, pulled the keys from the ignition and looked over at me. "You have some mouth on you, you know that?"

The way his gaze moved down my face, I knew he was going to kiss me.

TWELVE

❖

HE DIDN'T KISS ME. And I wasn't about to admit to myself how much that pissed me off.

Instead, he dropped the F-bomb, got out of the car (points for not slamming the door, though it seemed like he wanted to) and made his way to my side, opening the door for me. (Again, not yanking it open, but giving Yvette the deference she deserved.)

I got out of the car and he softly shut the door behind me, then showed me how to set her alarm system. While we waited for his ride to show up, he walked me around Yvette and pointed out different features as if he was a proud father bragging about his kid's little league scores.

I listened and asked questions, quickly becoming a proud mother.

I stuck my hands in my pockets, and he noticed and motioned me to him. When I reached him, he backed me into the side of the car and pulled my hands out of my pockets. He sandwiched them between his own, like we were doing some kind of group prayer or something. Then, ever so slowly, he moved his up and down over mine, causing the nicest friction. And heat. Heat that could make a girl forget it was early February and she'd forgotten her mittens in her dorm room.

And also forget just who was causing the oh-so-delicious

heat that was now spreading beyond my hands.

I would be wise to remember who Stick was. Is.

Yes, I had developed a hard shell and was pretty world-wise. But even though I was brought up in a world of power-hungry vipers, I hadn't been exposed to the criminal element much.

Well, yeah, I suppose I had…just of the very, very white-collar kind. And the kind that never get caught.

Starting to pull my hands away, knowing I needed to keep my distance—lovely heat or not—I looked up at Stick and met his gaze.

It was like he read my mind—knew the moment when I decided that he was not the type of guy I wanted.

That I thought I was too good for him.

"Fuck you," he whispered with not much accusation. More, almost, with a bit of hurt in his voice.

Which pissed me off. Yeah, maybe I did think he wasn't good enough for me, but he was a known car thief, for Christ's sake—that pretty much defined that he was not the route I wanted to take.

"No. Fuck you," I whispered back, no heat in my words, though I was pissed at him for his past. Pissed at myself for wishing he didn't have it. Pissed at life for putting us both in the positions we were in. Pissed at how much I wanted to feel his hands all over my body.

I yanked my hands away again, but he not only held on fast, he pulled my hands, arms and body into his. He took a step closer, then another, backing me up against Yvette.

"You don't know shit about me," he said softly.

"And I don't want to," I replied, though nothing was further from the truth. But even though I could be wild and outrageous, I did have a streak of self-preservation a mile wide. I'd had to.

He dipped his head slightly, even though I was shaking my head at him. Shaking that I didn't want him to. But I couldn't get the word "no" out. He nodded at me, and the corner of his mouth turned up into a grin just as I closed my eyes and he kissed me.

It wasn't a sweet, tentative kiss of two people just dating. It wasn't even the fun, exuberant kiss that he'd planted on me on the dance floor at Betsy's wedding.

It was mean. It was angry.

And it was something I completely understood and responded to.

His mouth demanded from mine, and I pushed back, opening my lips under his, letting his tongue in, tangling, twisting with mine.

He tasted like peppermint, and with the cold air swirling around us, it all felt like a winter wonderland.

But he was not the guy who should be making me think of lame phrases like "winter wonderland" while he kissed the bejeezus out of me.

And that thought should have made me pull away. Instead, I broke my hands free from his and wrapped them in the soft cotton of his hoodie, chest level, and yanked him even closer to me, needing to feel his body against mine.

His hands did the same, grabbing the lapels of my peacoat. He couldn't pull me closer—that was physically impossible— but he ground himself into me. My legs instinctively opened, giving him room.

"Christ, Jane," he whispered as we came up for air, "I don't even *like* you." He was kissing my jaw, which was about the only thing exposed given the high collar of the coat.

I barked out something between a laugh and a sob, hoping it sounded like a laugh. "And I think you're a complete asshole."

He pulled back, gazing at me with a look in his eyes that

I couldn't read, but made me uncomfortable. I moved my mouth back to his, resuming the kiss, wanting to block out his face. Block out his knowing look. Block out the thoughts and emotions swirling around in my nearly frozen brain.

And just feel the heat.

Our hands were touching again, backed up against the other's, each of us clutching clothes and trying to get closer.

His hips moved against mine, slow, easy. Nothing like the furiousness in our kissing.

It was like a challenge, combat almost—who could taste the other more, who could fit their lips the mostly perfectly against the other's. Who could make those delicious moans come forth.

I opened my eyes and saw our breath from our joined mouths float off in little clouds due to the cold. And I looked up and saw Stick staring into my eyes as he hungrily feasted on my mouth.

It was too close. And, delicious as the heat rushing through my body felt, it was all wrong.

I loosened my grip on his hoodie, turned my hands and pushed him away. It wasn't a gentle "no, honey, that's far enough" push. It was a "get the hell off me" push, and Stick stepped back, though still held my coat.

"Not gonna happen," I said in a calm, low voice that masked the yearning and heat I felt inside. I met his eyes and made my face turn to stone. It was a look I'd perfected over the years. A look that said I would absolutely not change my mind.

He let go of my coat and took another step back. His hoodie was low enough that it hid the bulge I'd just felt pushing against me. He ran a hand through that mop of hair of his while never taking his eyes from mine. I didn't break eye contact either.

Both of us were breathing heavily, and the little puffs of

breath carried between us, almost like thought bubbles in the comics.

He didn't even look when his friend pulled up right behind him in Stick's car and got out of the driver's seat. Stick had probably heard the car approaching (like a mother knows her baby's cry), but I hadn't.

Not saying a word to either of us, the friend moved around the car and got in the passenger seat.

Stick's breathing seemed to return to normal, while my chest (damn it!) was still heaving.

Without looking behind him, he took a step back and placed his hand on the opened door with complete accuracy.

Okay, the guy truly pissed me off, and kind of scared me a little, but that was a *very* cool move.

"I can give you another lesson on Thursday. Same time. Yes or no."

No. No, no, no, my self-preservation voice screamed inside my head.

"Yes," I said.

No look of triumph, no parting smile. Just a small nod, and he got in his car and drove off.

Well, I had to give Stick one thing—asshole or not, the guy could make an exit.

THIRTEEN

✦

IT WAS A RARE NIGHT that all three of us were in our dorm room together. We studied for a while. Syd came over and plopped on Lily's bed while Lily studied at her desk.

After a while, we all took off our earbuds and started talking.

You would think that three people who lived together wouldn't need to "catch up," but we did.

They'd both gotten to the room late. It was the afternoon Lily gave swimming lessons, and Syd was at one of her jobs.

Maybe I should get a job. I was handling school okay, didn't need a ton of time for studying. With Lily and Syd so busy, I had extra time on my hands.

But then I thought about my upcoming second driving lesson. And would there be a third? And even if there wasn't, I'd have more freedom having a car on campus. I could drive into Baltimore, or down to DC. Not that I would, most likely, but I *could*.

I hadn't planned on telling my roomies about the car just yet. It still seemed kind of unreal, but then I realized it had been kissing Stick and standing in front of Caro Stratton's house that had been the most unreal parts of the afternoon. Those two items I'd definitely keep to myself.

"So, my dad bought me a car. I got it today," I said after a lull in the conversation.

Lily rolled toward me in her desk chair. "No way. That's awesome. What kind?"

"A Corvette," I answered, almost sheepishly.

The look that crossed Lily's face was priceless. Like she was confused as to why I'd get *that* car, and yet didn't want to say anything in case I was a Corvette junkie or something.

"It wasn't my choice," I said. Lily gave me a knowing, almost sympathetic look, and I felt this twinge of betrayal toward Yvette. Stupid, I know, but I put my chin up and added, "But it grew on me."

"This just happened today?" Lily asked.

"Yes. When I came home from class."

"Did you take it for a drive?"

I shrugged, and busied myself with putting my books away so I wouldn't have to look at her while I answered. I didn't want to see their reaction, and more importantly, I didn't want them to read anything into mine.

"Sort of. It's a stick shift, and I've never driven one, so it wasn't much of a drive. But I got a little better by the time I was done." Which might have been the exact words I would have used to describe kissing Stick—it got better by the time we were done.

"You don't know how to drive a stick shift?" Lily asked, a touch of incredulousness in her voice.

"No," I said, a touch of defensiveness in mine.

"Do you?" Lily asked Syd, now thinking maybe she was the odd one.

"I don't even know how to *drive*," Syd said.

Lily looked at her, then waved her away. "That's right. You're from New York. Nobody knows how to drive there."

Syd opened her mouth to argue, but ended up just shrugging and asking Lily, "You do know how to drive one, obviously?"

Lily nodded. "My dad insisted I learn when I started driving." She looked away, and I could tell she was embarrassed. She knew neither Syd's nor my father would be giving their daughters driving lessons. Mine would never take the time, and Syd was cryptic enough about her home life that I assumed her dad wasn't in the picture. I mean, my dad *was* in the picture, but there was no way in hell he'd have given me driving lessons.

I could picture Grayson Spaulding, or maybe Lily's mom, taking her out in the family Lexus or something and teaching her how to drive a stick.

But it wouldn't have felt the same to her. The way it felt to have Stick's deep voice telling me when to shift, coaxing me into feeling Yvette's every need. His hand on my thigh, inching its way upward.

His lips crashing down on mine as he yanked my body into his.

I shook my head, as if trying to physically dislodge him from my brain.

Thankfully Syd brought my thoughts out of Yvette's warm cockpit and the parking lot's cold air, and back into our room by asking me, "So, like, it was just here when you got back from class? Did your dad bring it to you?"

Syd had seemed fascinated with the whole Joe Stratton thing after Betsy's wedding, and then my father announcing his candidacy. Then photos would be in *People* and other mags, and there I'd be, alongside my family, looking like I belonged.

The whole campus had seemed fascinated for about a minute. But Bribury was full of political and celebrity offspring, and it quickly died down, thank God.

"No. He had it dropped off. Somebody…else brought it over."

Syd nodded, but Lily looked at me strangely. Did she

already know about Stick through Lucas somehow? Or had there been something weird in my voice that she picked up on?

I cleared my throat. "Actually, that thug friend of Lucas's brought it over. We knew he could *take* cars. Apparently he can deliver them, too."

"Stick? Stick brought you your car?"

So she hadn't known. Damn, that meant she'd picked up on something else. God, did I have a Stick tell?

"And what? He just shows up with a car, hands you the keys and runs off? You must have been like…WTF."

Of the three of us, only Lily would use the letters instead of saying the words, but it made me smile that she did.

"No. He gave me a quick lesson on driving her. Then he left in his car, which a friend had followed him over in." All true. The definition of "quick lesson" probably wouldn't hold up under scrutiny, and they didn't need to know that the friend left for quite a while and then came back for Stick. But yeah, no lies or anything.

Lily eyed me suspiciously, but Syd was lying on her back on Lily's bunk and seemed not to pick up on anything.

Not that there was anything to pick up on.

"Well," Lily said, "if there's anyone to teach you how to drive, it would be Stick. That guy knows *a lot* about cars."

"One would assume that, given his nickname," Syd said, as she checked her phone, then laid it on top of her stomach and put her arms behind her head.

Don't ask, I told myself. *Do* not *ask*.

"Yeah, right. Hey, Lily, do you even know that asshole's real name?"

Yeah, I guess I did have a Stick tell. Lily rolled even closer to my bed, her eyes narrowing. "No, I don't. But I could find out if you wanted." She started to reach for her phone.

"No," I said, maybe a bit too forcefully. "Don't bother.

Who cares, anyway? I just thought Lucas might have called him by his name or something."

She took her phone from her desk but didn't do anything with it, just held it out, almost like she was daring me. "No, Lucas has always only called him Stick."

"I bet he calls him a lot more than just 'Stick' since he was arrested. Oh, wait, he probably doesn't even talk to the guy anymore."

Lily shook her head, confused. "Why wouldn't Lucas be talking to Stick? And he is. They're together all the time, when Lucas isn't working or…"

"With you," I said, nodding pointedly to Lily's bed, where Syd was texting on her phone, seemingly oblivious to Lily and me.

A flush came over Lily's perfect face. God, she even blushed beautifully.

I wasn't jealous of Lily's beauty often. I had come to terms with my looks—offbeat, quirky, but attention-getting—a long time ago. I'd had to own myself early on, or my mother would have created a mini-me, and there was no way I was going to let that happen.

"In fact," Lily said, "Lucas and Stick seem even tighter after the whole arrest thing."

"How can that be? Doesn't Lucas blame that asshole for even being arrested?"

"Maybe *that's* his real name…That Asshole. You sure call him that enough," Syd said, not taking her eyes from her phone. Apparently she *was* listening.

"Lucas doesn't blame Stick for what happened," Lily said.

"Why not? He should."

She shook her head. "That's not how he sees it. Lucas totally owns what he did."

"Well, yeah, he should. But he should still see who put

him in the position in the first place."

Lily shrugged. "I don't know. I don't know all the details of how it went down, but I know Lucas doesn't hold Stick responsible. At all."

She seemed so nonchalant about the fact that her boyfriend had a Past. I didn't want her to read anything into my question, but I had to ask. "How do you deal with the fact that Lucas has...done stuff in his past?"

A pained look crossed her face, which she quickly masked. So, not so nonchalant after all. "I don't know. It didn't seem to matter at first because it was all...crazy attraction, and just needing to be near him. I wasn't thinking long term enough to where his past, his life before me, would come into play."

She looked away from me, out the window, into the dark night. I noticed Syd's fingers stilled on her phone, and her head tilted in Lily's direction, watching.

"But then," Lily continued, "when I knew it was going to be something more, something...deeper, I had to really think about it. About how I would deal with it, how I would let it affect me."

"And?" I coaxed when she'd said nothing for a moment, just stared out into the night.

She turned back to face me. "And...I realized that, hokey as it sounds, his past was what made him who he is right now. Am I happy that he had a drug problem? No. Am I proud of the fact that he was involved with Stick's car theft operation? Absolutely not. Do I believe that both of those things are firmly behind him? Yes." She took a deep breath, then let it out. "Am I so deeply in love with him that I'm able to let go of his past? Absolutely."

"But what if you weren't as certain as you are that he'd put that all behind him? Could you still—"

"Are you saying it isn't? Do you know something about

Lucas? Did Stick say something—"

"No. No. Nothing," I said quickly, holding up my hand as if to stop Lily's panicking thoughts. "I'm sorry, that's not what I meant at all. I didn't mean to imply… That's not where I was going."

A look of relief came over her face, and I realized that no matter how much Lily trusted Lucas (and she did), and no matter how true it was that he was done with his past (and I believed it to be absolutely true), there would always be this tiny, minuscule part of her that knew it was there.

And it was so much larger with Stick, who was the freakin' mastermind of his little car theft ring.

Yeah, the look he'd read on my face today, the look that said I knew he was bad news, the one that had royally pissed him off, was one that would never go away.

Lily had learned to deal with it, to push it way, way to the back of her psyche.

But I knew there was no way that I could.

FOURTEEN

❖

"WANT A MINT?" Stick asked, holding a roll of peppermint Life Savers in front of me.

"Gimme a sec," I said, needing my hands to steer and shift Yvette down as we took a hill.

He gave a tiny snort of laughter. "Some day you'll be so good at this that you can hold a cigarette, a beer, unwrap a mint and downshift up a curvy hill, all at the same time."

"Um…there's so many things wrong with that sentence I don't even know where to start."

Out of the corner of my eye I caught his smile. He unwrapped the roll of mints, took one and held it in front of my mouth. I waited a second for him to make some crude comment about me opening up for him or something, but he just patiently waited. And when I did open my mouth and stick out my tongue, he just placed the mint on it, then took his hand back.

Not resting on my thigh as he had last time, but firmly back in his lap.

Not that I *wanted* his hand on my thigh. Just being in the small, cocoonlike cockpit with him was jarring enough after that angry kiss we'd left with on Tuesday.

But he hadn't mentioned the kiss when I'd met him outside my dorm, nor on the walk to Lot H, not even when we'd gotten out of town and he'd pulled over and we'd switched positions and I'd started driving.

In fact, it was like I was totally some driving lesson student and he was acting the professional teacher.

It was good that he'd decided to go this route.

And it drove me mad.

The scent of him—once we'd gotten into Yvette and the seat warmers and heater had been going—wafting through the small car. It was a mixture of laundered cotton, oil and peppermint. And it drove me crazy.

Now, tasting the mint he'd so carefully placed on my tongue, I knew at least where that part of the Eau De Stick had originated.

And I was reminded of the taste of him. The mint brought it all back, and I ground the clutch a little bit. "Sorry, baby," I whispered to Yvette, getting her back in gear.

Yeah, *I* needed to get back in gear.

I waited for Stick to make some smartass comment about the clutch, but he kept quiet. He did, however, place his hand on the dashboard, and I swear he petted her a little bit, as if to calm Yvette.

Damn, but I wanted him to pet me, too. Except that I didn't. Because I knew it wouldn't—couldn't—go anywhere. And I could get plenty of casual sex with my Bribury boys—I didn't need to seek out a townie for it.

Even though I figured Stick might know a thing or two more between the sheets than the rich boys on campus.

"Thanks for the mint," I finally said, desperate for something to say so I wouldn't blurt out something stupid like, "It tastes like you do."

"No problem. Anytime. I always have them on me."

"Oh?" I said, sounding like an idiot. Like I cared that he always had peppermint Life Savers on his person.

We were coming up on the town of Chesney, and I wondered if I should pull over and let Stick get us through the town and all its stoplights.

"Keep going, you're doing fine," he said, as if he read my thoughts.

At the first light I caught a red, and I stalled out when the light turned green. Cars beeped behind me, and I tried to cover how flustered I was, but Yvette knew, refusing to gently go to first. I suspected Stick knew as well.

"Take your time. Concentrate on Yvette. Fuck those yahoos behind us." His voice was low and strong, and even though it came from his side of the car and was not whispered in my ear, it gave me the steadying I needed, and I got her in gear and moved down the Chesney main street.

"Yeah, peppermints," Stick said as I made my way to the next light, which was also turning red, much to my dismay. I took a peek in the rearview mirror and saw all the same cars were still behind me. "I took 'em up when I first started smoking," Stick said as we glided to a stop at the light, my feet feeling like lead as I tried to keep my hand light and easy on the shifter, placing it in neutral. Even dangling my wrist off the knob as I'd seen Stick do, trying to fake it till I made it.

Wait, what? "You used to smoke?" I asked Stick, his comment finally permeating.

"Yeah, since I was twelve."

I looked over at him. "You started smoking at twelve?"

"Since eleven, actually, but not hardcore until twelve, yeah. Green light," he added at the end. "Smooth as silk," he said softly.

My mind was boggling on the eleven-year-old smoking bit. I mean, I'm not naive, but still, eleven years old?

I shifted into first and pulled through the green light. "Did your parents know you were smoking at eleven years old?"

I felt, more than saw, the shrug of his shoulder so close to mine, and yet not touching. "If they did, they didn't say anything."

Hardly one to comment on neglectful parenting, I kept my mouth shut.

"How long ago did you quit?"

It took him a few seconds, but he came back with, "Two years, four months and three days ago." He took another mint from the roll and popped it in his mouth, then returned the roll of candy to his front jeans pocket.

"Must have been pretty momentous for you, if you can rattle the exact date off so easily."

"It was also the day my father was diagnosed with stage four lung cancer."

"Oh. Sorry."

"Shit happens. Don't know what he expected, being a pack-a-dayer for thirty years."

"Yeah, that would do it."

"Yep."

"So…how long after the diagnosis…did he…"

"He actually hung on longer than you would have thought. Tough old bastard. I think he did it just to piss off the doctors who said he had a few months tops. He lasted a year."

"But probably not a great year…for any of you."

"No," he said very quietly.

"And your mom?"

"Not in the picture."

"During the cancer, or ever?"

"Ever."

God, how many times had I wished that one of my parents (and it rotated which one, but mostly my father) was just…out of the picture? That they simply didn't exist.

But was that really what I'd wanted? I guessed Stick would

have liked his mother during that last year of his father's life, even if he was, like, eighteen or nineteen himself.

"Do you have any sisters or brothers?"

"Nope, only child." He looked out the side window, his face away from mine so that I couldn't even catch a glimpse of it as I drove. "At least that I know of. I suppose my mom could have a whole different family out there somewhere."

"You never tried to find out?"

I saw the gentle shake of his head, his hair a tangled mess in the back. Did the guy even own a comb? And, okay, yes, it was sexy as hell all tousled and resting against the grey cotton hoodie, but still. Guy could run a brush through it every now and then.

"Nah. She didn't want me, I didn't want her." It sounded so matter of fact, but I was getting to know him a little bit now, and I called bullshit on his tough-guy words. But I kept my mouth shut.

"So, you were, like, the only one there for him that year? Or had he remarried?"

That got a genuine bark of laughter out of him. "God, no. He'd never take his head out from under the hood of a car long enough to even get a date, let alone get married again. It's a wonder he was even with my mom long enough to create me. She must have shown up at the garage or something." There was a tenderness, almost a jokiness in his voice as he said the last, and it made me smile. I was happy he was still turned to the window so he wouldn't see.

"Maybe she got on one of those wheeling thingies and slid under the car beside him," I said, playing along.

He laughed, an honest, pure, deep sound that made me bite down on my Life Saver, spreading peppermint coolness throughout my mouth.

"There's a dipstick joke in there somewhere, but it's not

coming to me," he said, humor still in his voice.

It felt good. It seemed that we were always either scrapping with each other, or having an awkward silence as we'd had so far today.

This joking—*with* each other instead of *at* each other—was an odd change, but it felt good.

"So, *you* were nurse? No lady friend to do it?"

"Right. Just me. His best friend tried to run the garage for him with my help, but after a while I didn't want to leave him alone for very long, and then I *couldn't* leave him alone, so I didn't go into the garage."

The humor was gone now, and I knew the rest of the story was not good. Well, I mean, obviously his father dying after a prolonged cancer battle wasn't good to begin with. But there was something...more.

"The garage," I said, almost to myself, like I'd found the missing piece to the puzzle.

"Yeah. It was losing money with my dad not being there. When he got an offer for it—a shitty, lowball offer—he said no at first. But the medical bills were piling up, there was no way we could pay them, even if Dad and I could both work full-time, which we couldn't."

"Of course not."

"So, when the offer came a second time—still just as shitty—he had to take it. It's almost a good thing he was dying. Giving up that place would have killed him anyway."

"Was it enough? For the bills? For his...treatment?"

"Not hardly. It helped. It made a dent. But it wasn't enough. And with no income from the garage coming in..."

"That's when you started stealing cars," I said, finishing what he probably wouldn't have said.

"Something like that." Denying to the end, but he was nodding. "See? Criminal with a heart of gold. Don't you feel bad now, always crawling up my ass about my lowlife-edness?"

"But you didn't stop after your dad died," I pointed out.

He waved a hand, but it fell to his lap without much oomph behind it. "Details."

Yeah, but a big detail. Stick liked the money even after his desperate need for it had been buried. Or the adrenaline. Or the power. Or the stealing-from-the-rich aspect. Whatever. He was still a car thief.

Okay, retired car thief.

"I'm sorry," I said again. "About your father passing, I mean." I didn't want him to think I had any sympathy for him turning to crime. That was on him.

Probably every townie had a sob story. I supposed that was why they became townies instead of college students.

He waved a hand of dismissal at my "sorry," and then motioned to the road in front of us—well out of Chesney, out on the country road and well past all the traffic lights behind us.

"You did good," he said. "After that first light, you were golden."

I looked at the road, stunned to see how far out of town I was. And how I hadn't even noticed each successive light we'd stopped at in Chesney. Each light that I'd apparently expertly stopped and driven through. Were we really this far out of town?

"What? Was that some kind of Jedi mind trick? Get me talking about your hard-luck story and I wouldn't freeze up at lights?"

"Worked, didn't it?"

Damn. It had.

We weren't far from the turnoff to the road that Caroline Stratton's house was on.

"So, want to make a return visit?" Stick asked. "You don't

have to just stare at the gates this time."

"What do you mean?"

"Caroline said to bring you up to the house if we were out this way again together."

"She did? She hates me."

"Didn't seem like it to me. And yeah, she said to come up and say hi."

"And you said we—I—would?"

"I didn't say. I honestly didn't know if we'd do this again. This was when I was in her house on Tuesday. When you were outside."

"Before we kissed" was what went unsaid. By both of us.

"Do you have to drop something off again? Return keys? Account for anything missing?"

"Ha. Ha."

I smiled, liking that the barbs had returned. It felt…safer, somehow.

"No, I don't have to drop anything off. But I should probably check in…on the garage."

"In case one of your competitors got word that you have a garage full of priceless cars?"

"They wouldn't dare."

I laughed. "That would be rich, though."

"Don't even joke about it." He ran his hand through his hair. "Shit. Now I really do want to check on the garage. Let's just stop in for a minute. You can say hi to Caro and I'll check on the cars. Everybody's happy."

I didn't counter with the fact that I didn't need to say hi to Caro Stratton to be happy, and I was willing to bet seeing my face was not going to make her day. Still, I took the turn and headed down the road that would bring us to her gates.

"Should we call first or something? It's pretty rude to just show up on her doorstep."

Stick fished his phone out of his pocket and texted…I assumed to Caroline.

And by the way, since when was Stick calling her "Caro" on a regular basis? That was something her family did. And I wasn't including me in that.

His phone pinged as I neared the Stratton estate. "All set. She says come on up." When we got to the gate, Stick told me the code and I punched it in.

I thought about all the times I'd been here with Pandora. I shuddered to think what might have happened if we'd had the code back then.

The gates opened slowly—tastefully slowly. I stalled out trying to ease Yvette up the drive.

"Maybe this isn't a good idea," I said. "Seems like Yvette knows I don't belong here."

"Do I need to come up with another tear-jerker, woe-is-me story to get you up this driveway? I'm fresh out, so you might as well pull over and we'll walk up the damn thing."

"Shut up," I said, and started the car up again, easing into gear much more smoothly. I sighed. Shit, would I always have to be emotionally moved by Stick—either in sympathy or rage—to be a good driver?

I finally pulled to the middle of the circle drive, right in front of the impressive, yet understated, home.

Some sick part of me wanted to do a selfie in front of it and text it to my mother, but I kept the urge in check.

I cut the engine, but kept my hands on the steering wheel.

Stick got out of his side, then walked around to mine. I wasn't waiting for him to open the door for me, I was debating starting the car back up and taking off.

As if he sensed it, he opened the door, reached in and took the keys out of the ignition.

"Come on, chickenshit, it's just one small lady in one big

house."

As he knew I would, I rose to his challenge, mentally and physically, rising out of the car and following Stick to the front door.

FIFTEEN

✦

"JANE, IT'S SO GOOD to see you. Please, come in," Caroline Stratton said, holding the enormous front door open for Stick and me.

Speechless, I shot a look at Stick. A "there will be hell to pay later" look that he totally understood.

He nudged me inside, following me. "I'll explain later," he whispered in my ear.

What Stick would need to be explaining, and what had me so shocked that I could barely walk into the grand foyer, was Caroline's appearance.

The woman, whom I had just seen at Betsy's wedding six or seven weeks earlier, had dropped at least thirty pounds since then.

And not in a good way.

The cancer was back. And if I had to guess (and that was all it would be, given my very limited knowledge of the disease), I'd say it was pretty advanced.

Caroline and Stick exchanged a look, and I knew it was about my reaction.

"Sorry for the intrusion, Caroline," I said. Meaning it even more so now that I'd seen her. She was dressed in a comfy-looking designer tracksuit that hung on her, but not as much as it should have. She'd obviously bought some newer clothes recently.

Or had someone buy them for her. There was no way she could have gone out looking like this and it not be all over the news.

So she had decided not to tell the public.

And why did I think that had something to do with my father running for governor?

"Let's go into the kitchen, shall we? I was just looking at the proofs the wedding photographer emailed. You look absolutely beautiful in them, Jane."

I followed her through the foyer, taking surreptitious glances into the rooms that we passed. A great room done in taupe and deep blue. A study, walls lined with bookshelves and a huge, but feminine, desk in the middle of the room, lots of comfy chairs with soft-looking throws laid over their corners. A formal dining room with heavy, dark furniture and floor-length windows that looked out onto the rolling grounds of the estate, bare and frozen.

And then the kitchen, which I entered behind Caroline. She went through the room and stood by the long granite counters, then waved me toward the sunny nook, where she had a laptop open, a cup of something by its side.

"We've disturbed you," I said, wishing I was anywhere but here. Curious as I was to see the inside of the house I'd stared at so many times, I felt like an intruder.

Which was exactly what I was. Exactly what I'd always been to this woman—an intruder who broke up her family.

"Nonsense. Like I said, I was just looking at photos. Sit. What can I get you to drink? Are you a coffee drinker like Stick? Or would you prefer some herbal tea with me?"

"Um…neither. Just a water, if that's okay," I said, making my way to the table. Stick, I noticed, placed his phone and Yvette's keys on a place on the counter that looked like it was made for just such a purpose. And that he'd done it many times.

Which would not have been the case if he was always in the garage.

"Sit down, Caro," he said. "I'll get it."

She didn't protest, and made her way over to sit at the table, across from me. He followed her over and took her cup after glancing in it. "How about a refill?"

"Yes, please," she said. Her body seemed to deflate then, once she was seated and Stick was taking over hosting duties. Like she had expended all her energy just answering the door and leading us to the kitchen.

She probably had.

We sat in silence while Stick puttered in the kitchen. He put the kettle on to boil, grabbed a mug from a cabinet and set it under the Keurig, which sat on the counter. No guessing where anything was. No fumbling through drawers or cupboards.

The guy knew his way around this kitchen.

"Take a look," Caroline said to me, turning her laptop around. The wedding photos were on the screen, and I scrolled through them. "Didn't he do a lovely job? I think he really captured Betsy's and Jason's…excitement, don't you?" she asked.

"They're really nice," I said honestly. Betsy looked beautiful, and Jason looked like a man in love.

I felt a pang somewhere in my throat, and I had to swallow before I spoke. "You look great," I added, a bit less honestly.

The Caroline in the photos looked tired now that I knew. Stylish and totally put together, but a bit ragged if you were looking for it, which no one was at the time. All eyes were on Betsy and Jason, and to a lesser degree…me. Or at least how the Stratton family interacted with me.

"It was a great dress. The shoes were killing me by the end of the night, though," she said, and I nodded my agreement.

"Mine too."

She turned the laptop back to face her, then patted the seat next to her. "Come sit here so we can look at them together."

I jumped at the opportunity to not have to face her. To not have to look at the loose skin and lined face.

She wore her hair pulled back into one of her famed chignons, but her hair was dull and listless and looked like it would be brittle to the touch. And much thinner than it had been at the wedding.

But not chemo thin. Not like it was falling out in handfuls. Not like it had years ago when she'd been doing major treatments.

She wasn't undergoing treatment. At least not chemo.

Sitting side by side, we scrolled through the shots. Stick put a bottle of water down next to me.

"A glass too, Stick," Caroline gently said, and he nodded and got a glass for me. He refilled her tea cup once the kettle whistled, placing a new bag in it. And he made himself a cup of coffee and then joined us at the table.

"I know some bridesmaid's dresses can be hideous, but I think Betsy picked out a beautiful dress. Did you like it, Jane? You certainly looked exquisite in it."

"I'd hardly say exquisite," I said.

"Know when to take a compliment," she said with a smidgen of teacher in her voice. The same tone she'd used on Stick about getting the glass.

I nodded. "Thank you. And yes, I did like the dresses." I thought about how the peach skirt of the dress twirled when I danced, and how much I'd liked how I'd looked in it.

I looked over at Stick, who was taking a sip from his coffee mug. It was as if he was remembering dancing too. A small, soft smile played at the corner of his lips, and he quickly covered it up with another sip of coffee.

"I'm glad you liked the dress. I can't tell you the number of weddings I stood in when I was younger where I absolutely hated the dress." She waved a frail hand. "Too many to remember, that's for sure."

"This was the first wedding I'd been in," I said, trying not to stare at the tininess of her wrist.

"I know it wasn't easy for you to even be there, Jane. But it meant so much to Betsy to have you be a part of it."

I knew the woman was sick, but... "Oh, come on," I said. "Let's not go *that* far."

She looked taken aback, and I regretted that I'd said anything.

Then she burst into laughter. "God, you're right. And what does it matter now, anyway? You're a smart girl. You always were." She looked at me and gave me what seemed like a nod of respect. "You're right, it meant nothing to Betsy. But it did mean something to your father."

I refrained this time from saying exactly what I thought it had meant to my father. But she knew that I knew.

"Well, it meant something to *me*. Something real. I know you're not my child, but you are my children's sister, my daughter's only sister. It meant something to me to see you standing up at that altar beside Betsy. And Joey."

She placed a finger on the screen of the laptop, tracing around Betsy, and then Joey, and then dragging her finger down the line to me. "Especially now," she whispered.

"How long do you have?" I said quietly.

She shrugged. The movement seemed so odd on her, so... un-Caroline. "Not long."

Stick stood up, his cup in hand. "I think I'll go check the garage."

"What's wrong in the garage?" Caroline asked, but she didn't look up at Stick—she was still looking at the photo of her kids. And me, their sister.

"Nothing, I think. But I just want to check on the cars." He looked at me pointedly. My earlier crack about his competitors stealing Caroline's cars must have gotten to him.

Good.

SIXTEEN

✦

HE LEFT THE HOUSE through a back door in the kitchen, and I was alone with Caroline Stratton for the first time in my life.

It should have felt weird—being in the house I'd stared at with my mother, sitting at the kitchen table sharing chitchat with the woman whose life my mother destroyed.

The woman who was dying.

"Is Joey coming back from Africa?" I asked.

Her finger on the photo moved back over to Joey's handsome face. "No."

"They must have ways to get ahold of him, even if cell coverage isn't available wherever he is."

"They have service. He calls every now and then. Mostly he just texts me pictures of the group he's working with. He's loving it."

"They wouldn't let him out of the program, out of whatever commitment he made, to come home to be with you?" That sounded barbaric. If Joseph Stratton didn't have enough pull to make that happen, Grayson Spaulding surely did.

"It's not that. He can leave at any time."

Something wasn't adding up. And the beginning of that odd equation began with Stick.

"And Betsy? Why isn't she here with you?"

"She and Jason are in Europe. Or Asia, I think it is now.

They're taking an extended honeymoon before they move to their place in New York and start new jobs."

I had known that. Joey had told me at the wedding. Both the big honeymoon and Joey's trip to Africa had the added benefit—or perhaps sole purpose?—of keeping them out of the country while their father ran for governor.

But surely they'd put up with the annoyance of the campaign to be with their mother when she was sick?

Unless…

"You haven't told them, have you?"

She didn't answer, just continued to trace her finger back and forth between her two children. I noticed her path didn't include me any longer, but just a glide back and forth between Betsy and Joey.

"No," she finally said. There was a finality, a steeliness, in her voice that told me nothing I said now would make any difference.

And I don't know what I would have said anyway. I was not part of this family, not Caroline's family, much as she tried to include me from time to time.

For whatever reason, she had chosen not to tell her kids she was dying.

"I'll tell them," she said. "I'll have them come back, when it's time. When I'm closer. I will…say goodbye to my children."

I wanted to ask when she thought that would be, but how do you ask that?

I took a drink of water, waiting for her to say more, but she didn't. She finally stopped looking at the photos, pushed the laptop away and took a drink of tea. She held the mug in her hands after she drank, elbows resting on the table, and stared out the window to the grounds of the estate.

We sat in silence, though not awkward silence, until I saw Stick coming back into view, presumably from the direction of the garage area.

As he entered, I stood up. "Well, we should probably get back. I've got some studying to get to."

She looked up at me from her seat, blinking several times, as if she was putting me in focus, trying to place me.

Had the disease settled in her brain?

"And how are you finding Bribury, Jane? Are you enjoying your freshman year?"

Okay, so she was still lucid.

"I am. Very much. I get along great with my roommates. I'm liking my classes for the most part."

She smiled, but it was a practiced smile and didn't quite reach her eyes. "That's nice. Bribury is a good school. You'll enjoy your time there. What are you majoring in?"

My pat answer for that was usually "partying," but I held it in check. "I haven't decided yet. I'm just getting in all the basics this year."

She nodded, looking away from me, back to the window. "That's a good idea. No need to commit to something right away." She looked back to me. "You'll find what speaks to you."

Would I? I wasn't quite as sure, but I knew I wasn't the only freshman in the world who didn't know what they wanted to be when they grew up.

Hell, I wasn't even the only freshman in my dorm suite who didn't know.

Stick poked his head in the fridge. "Can I make you something before we go?" he said. "How about an omelet?"

"I'm not hungry, Stick, thank you."

He shut the fridge door and gave her a stern look that I was willing to bet very few people gave to Caroline Stratton.

"When was the last time you ate, Caro?"

"Dotty made the most delicious crab salad for lunch."

"But did you eat any?" he asked with the suspicion of a

parent wheedling the truth out of toddler.

She looked away from him, just as a guilty toddler might, and shrugged. "A little bit."

"Where is Dotty, anyway?"

"Grocery shopping."

"How about a quick omelet? We've got time." He looked at me questioningly.

"Sure. We can stay," I said, and made my way over to Stick at the counter. I wasn't much of a cook, but I figured I could help with an omelet.

"Really, Stick, I can't eat anything right now. And Dotty will be home soon with enough food to feed an army. She'll make something mouthwatering for dinner, and I promise I'll eat."

He studied her, then finally gave one short nod. She exhaled, like she'd just been given a death-row reprieve.

"Are your omelets *that* bad?" I teased him under my breath.

He rolled his eyes at me, but moved away from the counter, toward Caroline. "Is there anything I can do before we leave?"

"No, dear, you do enough. We're fine today."

"And you're sure Dotty will be home soon?"

She nodded. "I think I'm just going to go lie down until she gets back."

"Okay. We'll show ourselves out." He gathered up his phone and my keys and motioned for me.

I walked over to Caroline. What was the proper etiquette here? Shake her hand? A kiss on the cheek? I felt like I might break some bones if I hugged her.

Not that she'd want a hug from me.

"Thank you for…the water," I finally said, making no move to touch her in any way.

She smiled softly, like she got how weird the whole situation was.

"You're very welcome, Jane. Feel free to stop by…for water anytime."

I smiled, but didn't quite laugh. It was all just so strange.

I turned to leave her, but she placed a cold hand on my sleeve. "I mean that. Please come by with Stick again. I enjoyed the company."

"I…I'm not sure…"

"I'll bring her by again," Stick said from behind me.

"Only if you want to," she said to me, a sadness in her eyes.

"That would be nice," I said. I leaned closer to her. "I only hesitated because I wasn't sure I'd need any more driving lessons from Stick."

"Oh, is that what brings you out this way? I'll bet he's a good instructor."

I thought of how he'd distracted me in Chesney with talk of his father so that I wouldn't freeze up at the traffic lights. He was a good instructor, but I wasn't going to give him the satisfaction of knowing I thought so.

"There's lots more I can teach you," he said. He was standing right behind me now, almost touching. He held out my coat to me, his arm brushing mine.

"You help a lady on with her coat, Stick," Caroline said in that teacher tone.

"She's fine," he said, and tucked my coat over my outstretched hand. "She's got two hands."

Caroline gave a long-suffering sigh, and shook her head at Stick, but there was warmth in her face, and this time her soft smile reached her eyes.

I put my coat on (just fine by myself, thank you very much), and followed Stick out of the kitchen.

At the doorway I turned back and looked at Caroline, still standing in the middle of the large room, looking small and frail.

I gave a tiny wave, which she returned.

"I'll come back," I said.

"Thank you."

I turned and walked out of the Stratton family home.

SEVENTEEN

❖

I LET STICK DRIVE HOME. He even tried to hand the keys back to me when I gave them to him, but I shook my head and moved to the passenger side.

It wasn't that I was mad, or so mad that I didn't want to drive. And I wasn't so overcome with emotion of the idea of Caroline Stratton dying that I wouldn't properly be able to shift Yvette.

I just felt kind of numb. Like everything I knew had been turned upside down.

Stick Whatever was apparently taking care of a dying Caro Stratton and she'd asked me to visit her.

Yeah, everything *was* turned upside down.

"Okay, spill," I said, after we'd cleared the town of Chesney and were heading back to Schoolport. We'd driven in silence since leaving Caroline's home.

"What exactly do you want to know?"

"Why you?" But the moment I asked the question, the answer came to me. "Because of your experience with your father."

"Yep. Grayson knew—somehow found out—about me taking care of my father. I actually got pretty good with it, administered IVs and shit. Even thought about doing it long term after he died."

"But by then you'd had a taste of the fast, quick money car stealing brought?"

He didn't look at me, just stared ahead at the bare road as he drove the deserted highway to Schoolport.

"It wasn't even that. It was more…" He gave a flip of the wrist that rested on the stick shift. "Never mind, it's stupid."

"I'm on a highway in a car I didn't want, with a guy I barely know, after visiting my mother's nemesis to find her dying of cancer." I took a deep breath, ran my fingers through my hair, tangling in the curls. "I think I can handle stupid."

He snuck a look at me and I gave him a "go on" nod.

"It wasn't the stealing of the cars. Yeah, sure, there's an adrenaline rush that comes with it. And, of course, the thrill of not getting caught."

"Of course," I said, like I knew what he was talking about.

"It was the info gathering I got off on. The making connections, forming the network."

I stayed silent, not really sure what he was talking about. I figured he just went up to a car and, you know…stole it.

"I built up the best group of sources around."

"I don't get it." He looked at me suspiciously. "Oh, come on, tell me. Who cares now, if you're really out of it," I added.

He made some kind of silent decision, took a deep breath and told me about his network of valets, cleaning people, gardeners, hairdressers—anyone who would know when people would be on vacation or away. He also knew about every high-end luxury or sports car that was purchased in a three-county area.

"I'd keep my eye on them all. And when we'd get a… request for a particular car, I'd know exactly where to go to get the information on when the car would be the easiest to… liberate."

I snorted at his word choice. But I had to say (although,

of course, I *wouldn't* say), it was pretty genius. Except… "Any one of those people could have turned on you."

"But they didn't."

"But they could have."

"Ah, but that's the risk you take. That's always the risk you take when you trust someone with your secrets, Jane."

I didn't touch that bait, just let it dangle on his pole.

"And these people were cool with you getting out of the biz? I'm assuming they were compensated for their information?"

"They were. Very well compensated."

"So they couldn't have been very happy about your newfound respectability."

"They weren't. Well, I think a couple were relieved. A few, the ones I thought were the best—I gave them the option of letting me pass their names on to…"

"On to who?"

"The people who requested the cars. The people that, in a way, I worked for."

"And I'll bet they were not pleased either."

I saw his hand tense on the gearshift knob, then soften, as if he feared hurting Yvette.

"You'd be right."

"No broken legs or anything?"

"Nah, not their style."

"What is their style?"

He shrugged. "It doesn't matter. It was unpleasant, but eventually they saw the value in me divulging my contacts. I only gave them a few at first, until I was sure that there would be no repercussions and they were sure they could trust my people."

"And this has all happened since the night Lucas was arrested? And you've become Nurse Nancy? Stick has been a very busy boy."

He rolled his eyes at me without looking my way. I could just *feel* it.

"Shortly after that night, yeah."

We rode in silence for a bit, entered Schoolport and took the turn off Main to head to campus.

I played it all in my head, the series of events that landed us here. "Why do I have the feeling that Grayson Spaulding played puppet master on all of this?"

"I don't know, why *do* you have that feeling?"

I sighed. "Oh, shut up. Tell me how he was involved."

"Shut up? Or tell you how Spaulding is involved? What's it going to be, Jane?"

He was infuriating. It was like dealing with a five-year-old. Except a five-year-old didn't make my insides squirm like they did now as Stick looked at me and grinned.

I quirked a brow at him and motioned with my hand for him to go on.

"Spaulding and I had a conversation not long after that. And somehow it came up about my experience with my father dying from cancer."

"*Somehow*?"

"You wanna hear or not?"

"Go on."

"Caroline was going to need help. And as you now know, she didn't want Betsy or Joey changing their plans just to be with her."

"They would want to know."

"That's what I told her early on. And she agrees when it gets…closer, she'll tell them."

"That's what she said to me, too."

He nodded. "She promised. I made her promise. I told her that as hard as that year was, I was glad I was able to be there for my dad."

He seemed embarrassed that he said that last part, and quickly went on. "Anyway, they didn't want the news to get out yet. Wanted to keep it controlled."

"Because of the campaign?"

"That, and the kids. And she really just wants to keep it private."

I thought about her previous fights with the disease and how they'd been all over the papers. The first time it was shown in a sympathetic light, as she and Joe Stratton battled the disease together while he was a senator and then presidential candidate. The second time was just after their divorce, and it was used to vilify my philandering father.

Rightfully so. But I could see how she'd want this to be out of the public for as long as possible.

"Restoring the cars is real, and I *am* working on them, but they won't take much. Her old man kept them in pretty good shape, actually."

"But it's your cover for being there." It wasn't a question.

He nodded. We reached campus, and he drove toward the student parking lot.

"And the wedding? Were you already working for her then?"

"No. That was my…audition, I'd guess you'd call it. How I could deal with that kind of group. Would I, I don't know, pull my junk out and piss all over the bride, or something?"

I laughed. "They wanted to see the animal in an unnatural habitat and see how he did?"

"Yeah, exactly."

I totally got that. That was kind of what everyone was waiting for me to do—show my true, low-class, daughter-of-a-home-wrecking-whore colors.

"And that kiss you laid on me on the dance floor?"

He smiled. "You know what? I kind of think that sealed

the deal for Caro."

"Does she have lots of visitors? Was that why it was important to make sure you could fit in?"

"That was the thought, but turns out she really doesn't have all that many visitors. I'm not sure if she's turning down offers because she's afraid word will get out, or…"

"If she's not getting any offers."

"Exactly."

"And Dotty? I'm assuming she knows?" I spoke the name like I knew Caroline's long-time housekeeper. I'd never met her, though she'd been at the wedding, crying the whole time over "Miss Betsy" being so beautiful.

But I remembered many a time my mother would scream into the phone at my father that she needed help. And it would almost always end with, "I need my own Dotty!"

He'd hired cleaning ladies for my mom, who came twice a week, but none of them ever lasted very long.

"Anybody else helping out? Home nursing of any kind?"

"Too risky that they'd tell the press. I *am* the home nursing. At least for as long as I can maintain. If it gets too bad, we'll call someone in. She won't be…in pain, if I can help it."

"You like her," I said, studying him.

He shrugged. "She's okay." The tone of his voice, though, assured me I was right.

"Who's to say *you* won't go to the press? Bet there'd be a lot of money for that story. The first picture of an emaciated Caroline Stratton would fetch top dollar."

"First of all, thanks for thinking that I'd be that low. Christ."

"Can you blame me? You are—were—a thief."

"That's different." I lifted a brow at that, but just motioned for him to go on. "Second, it seems Spaulding recorded a conversation I had with him about Lucas's arrest, where, shall we say, I *allude* to my possible involvement."

"He blackmailed you into doing this?" It didn't surprise me at all, except that it was a big risk for Grayson to take. Stick was a wild card, and I wasn't at all sure that he would respond well to coercion.

"No. I'd already agreed to do it before he told me about the recording. That's just insurance to him. *I* knew I would never do something that sleazy. Now he feels safe too."

"Why are you doing this at all? No matter what they're paying you, surely you would have made more stealing cars."

"There's a shelf life on that kind of existence. And I like my freedom."

"So you don't think you're one of the crooks that's too smart to get caught."

"Nope. A million things can happen during any... *transaction*, and almost all of them are going to do you in. This gig came along at the exact right time for me."

"Gig. Like it's playing in a club with your band or something."

He turned into Lot H, and I saw his car in the corner where Yvette had been parked. It hadn't been there earlier. He must have had someone drop it off for him while we were at Caroline's.

He pulled Yvette in next to his car and cut the engine.

"You know you can't tell anyone, right?" he said.

"Who would I tell?" I said. Just as I said it, my mother's face flashed in front of me. Oh, man, she'd *die* for this kind of information. Okay, bad word choice.

"I won't tell her," I said. "Anyone. I won't tell anyone."

"Nobody," he warned.

"I won't."

He studied me for a second, then nodded, as if he was convinced.

Then his eyes dropped to my mouth. He ran his hand through his hair, looked away and out to the parking lot.

"Damn," he said.

"What?"

He looked back at me as he said, "I swore to myself I was going to keep my hands off of you."

And then he put his hands on me.

EIGHTEEN

∗∗∗

I COULD HAVE stopped him.

There was a second or two, which seemed so much longer, as he moved his head to mine, as he lined up our mouths, as I felt his warm breath mingling with mine.

Yeah, I could have stopped him anywhere in there. Pushed him back, turned away, even gotten out of Yvette.

But I did none of those things. Instead, I leaned closer, letting the console push into my hip as his mouth came down on mine.

His usual peppermint taste mingled with coffee this time. Dark and rich yet fresh and light, all at the same time.

The thought that I knew what constituted a different taste of Stick, and how bizarre that was, briefly ran through my mind before he placed his hand along my jaw and deepened the kiss.

Then I lost all thought.

But I could feel.

And I felt the tug of his lips on mine, the way they fit, not perfectly with mine, but in a…quest. Almost a desire to conquer.

I totally got it. Because I felt it too. Not wanting to want like I did. Not wanting to enjoy the play of our tongues as they tangled. Not wanting to moan in delight when he pulled my lower lip with his teeth.

Not wanting Stick.

And yet…God, how I wanted him.

My hands fisted in his hoodie, pulling him closer. As close as the small car—and the seemingly huge console that divided us—would allow.

"Jane," he murmured, a whisper on my lips, and then he kissed me again, deeper. Even more desperately. And again, I got it.

It did feel desperate, like a losing battle to fight how good—how soooo good—it felt to kiss Stick.

He wasn't trying to conquer me. He was trying to conquer this feeling. He didn't want to feel it any more than I did.

I sucked on his tongue and he moaned, his fingers pressing into my jaw line, making me open my mouth even more to him. His thumbs brushed my cheeks, soothing, giving, while his mouth did nothing but take.

And I gave. Willingly.

We went on, tasting, kissing, gasping for breath when needed. At some point I noticed Yvette's windows were completely steamed up, and it felt like we were drifting in our own Corvette cockpit cloud. That the world, with car theft rings, and women wasting away of cancer, was so, so far away.

I tried to get to him, needing to feel his arms around me, wanting the comfort I knew that would bring.

And that thought was what pulled me away, both of us gasping, his hands reaching to pull my face back to his, but me sitting back in my seat, turning away from him.

Because I would find no comfort in Stick. He wasn't just some guy you could bang after a party for the pure physical pleasure of it, and walk away like nothing happened.

On the surface, yeah, that was exactly the guy who Stick should be.

And yet he wasn't.

"I told you," I said, facing out the side window. "We can't happen."

He would think it was because I had a hang-up about who he was, where he came from. What he did. And I'd let him think that—it served my purposes.

And maybe it was about that at first, certainly the other day it was.

But it was about more now.

Knowing about his father. Seeing him with Caro. I was dangerously close to...*liking* Stick. And that simply could not happen.

I wasn't a control freak or anything, but I'd watched my mother drive herself crazy wanting a man that she couldn't have.

And somewhere deep inside of me, a voice was telling me that I could never truly have Stick. That he was not the type of guy to go along with me just because I wanted him to. And I needed that. I needed to be in control of that aspect of my life. Because so much of my life I had no control over.

And hard as I'd tried to carve out my own little world here at Bribury, it seemed I was still surrounded by my father's enclave.

"Yeah, I know," was all he said. There was no defensiveness in it. No "fuck you," like the other day when he'd correctly read my thoughts about him. "That's why I told myself to keep my hands off of you," he added, a resignation in his voice. And also a bit of failure.

"But you didn't," I said, then turned back to face him. His eyes roved over my face, then settled on my lips, which felt puffy and well used. I put my fingers on them, not knowing if it was to create a barrier, or to feel the effect his kisses had on me.

Not that I needed any reminder of that—I wasn't sure I'd

even be able to rise up out of Yvette, my legs felt so weak and trembly.

"No, I didn't. And I can't seem to say 'sorry' about it, either."

I nodded. I wasn't sorry he'd kissed me, either. "But no more," I said firmly.

"Right. No more," he agreed. We looked at each other for a second, then both nodded, like it was a handshake on our deal.

He opened his door, the cool air rushing in, almost pulling me out of my make-out haze. Almost.

"Next Tuesday?" he asked.

I nodded, and he shut the door behind him, got into his own car and drove away.

I sat for a very long time before I left Yvette and walked back to my dorm.

NINETEEN

✦

VALENTINE'S DAY was that weekend. Lily had a date with Lucas, so Syd and I had planned to go to a party wearing semi-slutty red dresses, and looking to hook up.

But at the last minute, she had to work, so I sat in our room and studied, even read ahead for a couple of the classes.

I could have gone out with others. Girls from our floor were always popping over and inviting us out.

Well, inviting Lily out. She was the most like all the other girls here. But Syd and I came as part of the package deal, so they invited us too.

But Syd was not "Bribury material" to many here (snobby bastards), and I kind of scared a lot of the other girls away. Probably because I called people out on their bullshit.

And there was a lot of bullshit at Bribury.

So I stayed in, and kept my fingers away from my phone.

It wasn't like I'd actually text Stick to see what he was up to, but I did keep the phone on the other side of the room, out of easy access.

And yes, I did nearly twist my ankle jumping up to get to it when it buzzed.

But it was only Lily saying she wasn't coming home and to not worry. Lucas was still staying with his mom and little brother to help out with the rent, so I knew she wasn't staying there with him.

They'd probably gotten a motel room somewhere. Or Lucas had taken her to the apartment he'd shared with Stick until last fall, when he'd moved to his mother's apartment.

I wanted to text and ask where she was, but I didn't. I wanted to take Yvette for a drive, but it was snowing out, and I hadn't driven her on snow yet. I started to text Stick that it might be a good time for a lesson with the new snow, but deleted it before I even finished.

It wasn't like me to just sit in the room when I wanted to be out, doing something—anything.

But there were a whole lot of things I was doing lately that weren't like me.

Find her. Be her…and let the rest of the bullshit go. Montrose's words came back to me again.

The guy was like some Buddha or something. I even considered downloading his oh-so-acclaimed novel and reading it, but in the end I just lay on my bed and stared up at the ceiling.

I must have drifted off to sleep at some point. Around four a.m. I heard Syd in the bathroom. She took a long shower, and when she'd been done for about ten minutes, I got out of bed, grabbed my comforter and made my way to her room.

"Hey," I said as I entered the room. I moved to the empty bed her former roommate Megan had used.

Megan had gone home to Nebraska after the first week because her mom had died. She'd thought she'd be back for this semester, but she didn't show in January.

Syd might still be in touch with her, but I wasn't.

"Hey," Syd said, her back to me. She was fiddling with something on her desk. "Sorry I woke you."

"You didn't. Or I don't think you did."

She looked over her shoulder at me, saw me still dressed

in leggings and a sweatshirt, not my pajamas. "Were you out?"

I shook my head as I sprawled out on Megan's bed, wrapping my comforter over me.

"No, I stayed in."

"Sorry I had to work," she said. She left the desk and went over to her bed. She'd thrown on her pajamas after her shower and put her long black hair into a wet ponytail.

"Lily with Lucas?" she asked. I nodded. "That's nice, that he was able to get Valentine's off and that they can be alone together."

"I guess."

She sighed, stretched out on her back, flinging her arms over her face. "It's so easy for them, hey? They both know they love each other. There's no drama. No should-they-or-shouldn't-they. It's nice, right?"

Syd hadn't been a fan of Lily being with a townie at the beginning, so her words were surprising. And a bit uncharacteristic.

"Well, it wasn't easy at first, remember?"

She waved a hand, as if Lily's broken heart at having to break things off with Lucas had been a minor hiccup. In a way she was right.

But I'd shared a room with Lily when she'd cried herself to sleep. I'd seen—more so than Syd—how devastated our friend had been until she'd worked things out with Lucas.

And it had scared me.

At the time, I'd filed it away—with my mother's perpetual desperateness—as two places I never wanted to end up.

I would not be the type of woman who was desperate to keep her man. So desperate she'd do anything. And I would *never* fall apart over losing a guy the way Lily had.

I didn't think less of Lil for it—I felt deeply for her. But I just knew that would never be me.

"But it was never because she didn't trust her feelings, right? It was just shit that got in their way," Syd said, still covering her face.

If I'd been more on my toes, I'd have been suspicious of Syd's mood and the things she was saying. Normally I would have pushed and prodded, and gotten to what Syd was *really* saying.

But I was distracted with her words as they applied to me. And my feelings for Stick.

It was time to stop denying that I wanted him to kiss me, that I felt something for him. But I wouldn't romanticize it and put it in a "Lily and Lucas" kind of love category either. Stick pushed my buttons, and I liked it. It was as simple as that.

And I very much liked when he kissed me—hard.

But that was all it could ever be—some stolen kisses, maybe a little more. Hopefully a little more.

I would never put myself in the position my mother had for all those years—begging for crumbs from a man. Or where Lily was now—helplessly in love.

"It's just so hard, you know," Syd said. I don't know if she was talking about anything in particular, but I murmured my agreement.

We lay in silence for a bit more, then I got up to make my way back to my room.

At the door, I saw a beautiful scarf lying over Syd's coat on the back of a chair. It was brightly colored and expensive looking, and did not at all look like something Syd would pick out. She was all about blending in, trying to look like the Bribury Basics. And this scarf stood out.

I bet it looked great on her, though, with her dark coloring.

"This new?" I asked, holding up the scarf.

She peeked out from under her arms and nodded. "Just got it." She kept her arms down, propping herself up on her elbows, watching me as I held up the scarf. It wasn't quite a paisley pattern, nor floral. It was really unique, like nothing I'd seen before. I did most of my shopping in thrift stores and consignment shops, loving older, funky, retro stuff. But I'd also had to tag along with my mother to enough high-end stores in Baltimore to know that this was quite a scarf. "It's beautiful," I said, meaning it. It wasn't something I'd pick out, but I could certainly appreciate it.

"Thanks," she said. Her eyes followed the scarf as I held it up to the light, then draped it back over her coat on the chair. I couldn't quite read her expression—kind of pensive, like maybe she'd spent way too much money on it or something.

"Good thing you picked up a second job," I said as I turned to leave.

"Yeah, good thing," I heard her say quietly, more to herself, as I walked out of her side of the suite.

TWENTY

※

IT BECAME A STANDING THING. We'd meet in Lot H, Stick would be standing next to my car or sometimes sitting in it with the engine running if it was cold, I'd drive Yvette to Caroline's house, where we'd spend a few hours, then we'd come back.

It moved from Tuesdays and Thursdays to almost every weekday. I started bringing my laptop and books and studying, either at the kitchen table with Caro nearby doing stuff on her laptop, or sometimes, if she was napping, I'd take my books to the garage and study while Stick worked on the cars.

Well, on those days, I mostly watched Stick as he moved with grace and skill around the fleet of vehicles. He was definitely in his element.

Some days, if he got particularly dirty, he'd go over to the guesthouse and shower before we left. He kept a few changes of clothes in the detached guesthouse. He said he'd even started spending a few nights a week there, just in case Caro needed him. The plan was that he'd eventually move in if—when—the time came.

Dotty lived in, but Caro had gotten so weak that she now slept in a bedroom on the main floor. I'd asked her if it was time to call back Betsy and Joey yet, and she said no. I didn't push it.

So, yeah, it was a nice little routine. Kind of my *Tuesdays with Morrie*, except it was nearly every day, and it encompassed not only Caro, but Dotty and Stick as well. Many days we'd just spend talking, careful to avoid tender subjects like my mother.

It seemed Caro was in the process of going through the kids' photos, with the idea of putting them in albums, but that never seemed to happen. She and Dotty would start to reminisce about the day such-and-such had happened with each picture.

But that was probably more important than organizing the pictures—*reliving* the pictures.

Reliving her life.

It felt odd seeing the pictures. Seeing the life I almost lived. The life I never could. And yet I was fascinated by them, too.

Dotty was suspicious of me at first, but warmed up after a few visits. Most times, she'd take advantage of our visits to go grocery shopping or run errands or something, never wanting to leave Caro home alone.

And yes, I started calling her Caro, after she'd asked me to. It felt odd at first. I'd so often heard my mother say, "that fucking Caro" that I stumbled the first few times. And then, like the whole surreal situation, it started to feel natural.

I hadn't told Lily or Syd about my sojourns to Chesney. They both worked during the late afternoons, so it wasn't obvious to them that I wasn't around.

I don't know why I didn't say something to them. Partly, I guessed, because I'd have to tell them about Caro's health, and I wouldn't do that. But I also sensed they'd read more into it than there was.

Or more than I wanted to admit there was.

Another part of the routine was the kissing. It was as if turning off Yvette's ignition after we were parked in Lot H was some kind of starting gun going off, the way we'd be at each other the second it happened.

Sometimes I'd reach for him, sometimes he for me. Most times it was hard to tell who moved first. We'd kiss for half an hour, longer. It was always too long, and it was always not long enough.

Yvette, champion chaperone that she was, prevented things from going any further, though there was some furtive groping—on both our parts.

As sleek and cocoonlike as each side of the cockpit was, it was hell to try and make out in.

"Why did you choose a Corvette," I'd moaned more than once into Stick's mouth as he kissed me when I'd try to get closer to him, only to be thwarted by the console and stick shift.

"Right now, I have no fucking idea," he'd say, and keep kissing me senseless.

When we were at Caro's, or even on the drive to or from, we were our usual selves—trash talking and constantly bickering.

Except when I'd go to the garage while he was working. He'd be mellow there, humming while he worked, a quizzical look on his face as he studied a car. A smile spreading wide as he would solve whatever mystery that car held for him.

It was too pure for even me to want to muddy up with insults, and I'd leave him alone, content to watch him in a place he belonged.

It occurred to me more than once that I had no such place. Never had.

I think it was the pool for Lily. I'd seen her swimming, and just after she'd be done. It was the same look of…completeness that Stick had when he worked on cars. He even had it when he was helping Caro.

But the kissing…that was definitely the best part of our

afternoon jaunts.

Eventually one of us would come to our senses and end it. And then a little trash talk would fly, usually followed by a curse or two (by both of us).

And always—*always*—when he would get out of the car, he'd lean back in, look at me and say, "Tomorrow?"

I would nod and he would leave. And I would walk to my dorm room swearing to myself that I wouldn't let it happen again.

But it always did.

SPRING CAME EARLY to the area, and by the first week of March I was roaring Yvette up and down the backroads by Caro's estate.

"Why'd you get me a stick, anyway? Why not just an automatic?"

"Because the manual transmission gives you torque."

"Whatever that is."

He sighed. "Yeah, just trust me. You want torque. Especially now that the snow is behind us."

"Hopefully."

"Yeah."

But it had been a low snowfall winter for us, and it had never deterred me, though the first time I'd driven Yvette in the snow Stick had given me pointers about how to handle her.

Now I raced Yvette up and down the road a few times, reveling in the feel of her. How she knew me, and I knew her. It was like Stick had first said—I got so I knew what she needed.

And she needed to go fast.

"See? That's torque," he said as I peeled out of first and took the deserted road once more.

"I like torque," I said. Stick laughed, and I couldn't hide my smile. "Soon we'll be able to put the top down."

"That'll give the students walking from Lot H quite a show," he said.

I didn't bother saying that wasn't going to happen again—we'd both know I was lying.

When we pulled through the gates to Caro's house, I immediately saw two vehicles parked in her circular drive.

"Oh, shit," I said.

"Why? Whose cars are those?"

"Well, one looks just like the Caddy that Grayson Spaulding was driving when he picked up Lily at Christmas."

"Oh."

"And the other is definitely my father's."

"Oh, shit."

"Yeah. Should we just keep going? Not stop?"

"No. I don't want them giving Caro a hard time about the campaign or anything."

"Do you think that's why they're here?"

He shrugged. "I don't know. I just know she shouldn't be alone with them in her current state."

He'd gotten very protective of Caro, and I had to admit I admired it in him. And, in a sick way, was kind of jealous of it. Pathetic to be jealous of a dying woman, I know.

I parked the car, and reluctantly followed Stick into the house. I could hear voices coming from the dining room, a room I'd never even been in.

When we entered, we saw it was indeed Grayson Spaulding and my father. They were seated at the table with Caro, Grayson at the head. Laptops were open in front of all three of them, mugs and empty plates were at each place and papers were strewn all over the massive table. There was even a big whiteboard placed on a portable easel with a bunch of diagrams and a calendar on it.

"Ah, just the person we need," Grayson said as we entered

the room. I looked to Stick, who shrugged.

"Jane, it's time to get you involved," my father said, flashing me his best politician smile.

My hands began to tingle with dread as I stepped into the dining room and took my seat at the table.

TWENTY-ONE

THERE WAS AN EMPTY SEAT next to my father and one next to Caro. Grayson read my mind and quirked a brow at me. Already the power play had begun.

I moved to Caro's side of the table and sat next to her. Grayson gave me a knowing look, and my father pretended that he didn't notice. And maybe he didn't. Maybe he left things like that up to Grayson.

Caro smiled warmly at me. "How are you today, Jane? Your Econ quiz go okay?"

I nodded. "Yes. Aced it."

"Good for you," she said, placing her hand on mine and giving it a squeeze.

Caro had been very nice to me these past weeks, and we'd talked about a lot of things. I would even say we'd grown quite close. But she wasn't a toucher. In fact, I think this was the first time she'd touched me.

It did not escape my notice that it happened for the first time in front of my father and Grayson.

They noticed too. My father gave a small smile, like he was happy I'd become so close to his ex-wife.

Grayson eyed Caro suspiciously.

"We're trying to figure out what might be best for Joe's campaign as it applies to my...involvement. And yours as well," she said, ignoring Grayson's look and giving my hand another squeeze before returning hers to the tablet and pen in front of her.

"Then it's probably a good thing I'm here," I said, looking pointedly at Grayson. He and I had not finalized any kind of deal about how much I'd be available for my father's campaign. Yvette was an opening bid, sure, but there was still negotiating to be done.

I scooted my chair up closer to the table, took off my coat. pulled my laptop, a notebook and pen out of my backpack, and placed them on the table.

"Okay, let's talk about it," I said.

"Can I get anyone anything?" Stick said, still in the doorway. "Caro? More tea?"

He made his way around the table, collecting empty plates and mugs.

"Dotty can do that, Stick, you don't need to."

"It's fine. Tea?" He picked up her empty mug.

"Yes, thank you."

"Sure thing." He was just about out the doorway when my father said, "More coffee for me, please." Stick kept walking. I wasn't sure if he'd heard my father or not. Or, more likely, he'd heard him but pretended not to.

We talked for a bit about my class schedule and how much I'd be available until school got out. It was assumed I would be part of the campaign full-time during the summer break.

"What if I'd wanted to get a job?" I said.

"Is your mother not passing on the money I send her for you? You don't need a summer job."

I had no idea how much he was giving my mother, and what percentage of it was being put into my account by her, but no, I didn't need money, and I said as much.

"Then I don't understand," my father said. "Why would

you want to get a job?"

I shrugged. "Responsibility, accountability…you know, all that grown-up shit that I'm supposed to be learning."

Stick was back with Caro's tea and a bottle of water, which he placed in front of me.

"I was thinking I might stay here for the summer, get a job and take a few extra classes." I hadn't thought any such thing until that moment, but it was awesome watching everybody's reactions.

Stick's hand stayed on the water bottle in front me, flexing just a tiny bit. He then removed it and stepped back, behind me.

My father looked confused.

Caro and Grayson shared the same look. One that said the bargaining was just beginning.

"How are you enjoying your new car, Jane?" Grayson asked, throwing the first volley.

"Considering I didn't ask for it, didn't want that kind and couldn't drive a stick shift…I like it just fine."

"Would you like a different make? That can be arranged." This from my father. He was looking over my shoulder, at Stick, giving him a "what a fuck-up" look.

"Actually, turns out it was the perfect car for me," I said. "I just never asked for one."

"What kid doesn't want a new car?" my father asked.

"The kind of kid who wants to bargain for something else," Grayson said.

There was a small snort from Stick, which he quickly covered with a fake cough. "If you don't need anything else, *Caro*," he said, and I imagined him staring down my father as he said Caro's name, "then I'm going to hit the garage."

"Why don't you stay?" Grayson said. "You might have a good understanding of what Caro would feel up to." He waved at the chair next to me, and Stick, after receiving a nod from Caro, sat next to me.

Now it looked like three against my father, with Grayson being the referee.

"You don't think I'm the best person to say what I'm able to do?" Caro asked Grayson with an iciness in her voice.

"No," he said, then looked back at this laptop.

I imagined this scene, or something similar, had played out around tables with these three for years before I was born, and for quite a few after. Even after the divorce.

Minus the dying of cancer, though that had been present before.

And certainly minus the bastard daughter sitting in.

Caro and Grayson would plan and plot, sometimes in sync, many times not. And my father would sit and listen… and let them try to make him king.

My mother's voice came back to me: *The only reason he was ever with her—the only reason he's still with her—was because she was almost as good a political mind as that prick Grayson Spaulding. He should have just hired her, not married her. But no, he had to hedge every bet and marry her for her father's connections.*

She'd had lots to say about my father choosing to stay with Caro even after I was born. Stuff you probably shouldn't share with a kid, but that never stopped my mother. To her, Joe staying with Caro and not wanting to be with my mother had always been about image.

"We just don't want you to overdo it, Caro," my father said.

"You just don't want me to keel over when you happen to be standing next to me."

She totally emasculated him, Jaybird. No wonder he went looking. No wonder he fell so fast and hard for me. That's the key, Jaybird, you have to soothe *them. Even if they're being total dipshits, you have to pretend everything they say and do is golden. That's how you keep a man."*

Never mind that Caro Stratton kept her man for twenty years before my mother came along, and my mother had never managed to keep any man for more than a year or two, including my father. Especially my father.

"Caro, that's not true, I—"

"Let's cut to the chase, shall we? I find that dying gives me a sense of urgency I'd rather not ignore."

"Okay, let's not pussyfoot around," Grayson said.

They'd been pussyfooting thus far? I couldn't wait to see how they acted when the gloves came off.

Except I could. I didn't really want to see these people interacting with each other as they normally did.

I'd kind of grown a grudging respect for Grayson Spaulding after Betsy's wedding. My father, though he hadn't earned my respect, was someone I was able to deal with.

And even after years of hearing my mother bad-mouth her, and having no illusions that she could be an ice queen at times, I'd grown to like Caro while watching her sift through the photos of her children.

I'd always respected her, been in awe of her, but now I liked the woman herself.

"Does the public knowing that I'm dying help you or hurt you?" Caro said. She directed this more to Grayson.

He shrugged. "It depends. And really, it could go either way. It could help with a sympathy vote. You and Joe have always shown a united front, been very upfront about co-parenting"—he waved a hand—"all that shit." Caro and my father were nodding along with Grayson. Stick and I stayed silent, but I sensed him fidgeting beside me. This was new to both of us, but at least I was genetically predisposed to be a dispassionate cutthroat.

"You would obviously be openly supportive of Joe running for office." He tapped his pen, looked around the table. "But… it could go the other way. Voters skew older, especially here, and people have a long memory. They might somehow equate you being sick with Joe cheating on you."

"That's absurd," my father said.

"It's a gut reaction. They wouldn't logically believe that. But they'd see you two together, obviously note that Caro was dying."

I looked out of the corner of my eye at how Caro was taking the frank talk, but she was nodding, and even finished for Grayson: "And emotionally make the leap from the man who hurt me to the state I'm in now."

"Right. It's a risk. But it's probably more of a risk to not have you public at all. It will open a can of 'what's Caro think about Joe running' that we'd do well to get out in front of."

"You sure we can't call Betsy and Joey back sooner?" my father asked Caro. "They'd help diffuse it all. If they were there too, supporting me and beside you, maybe people wouldn't make that emotional leap."

"No. I do not want them back until either after the election, or when I…need to say my goodbyes."

I could tell my father wanted to argue with her, but he wisely kept his mouth shut. His douche meter ticked lower by a few notches.

But he was still in the red zone.

Grayson was watching me, waiting. He knew it had to be my idea, even though he'd planted the seed at Betsy's wedding. I took a deep breath, and he gave me a small nod.

"What if I was there? Whenever Caro was? I mean, surely she's not going to—won't be able to—do a ton of stuff, right? A few appearances?" I motioned to Grayson. "You said something about an interview early on with a friendly journalist? What if I was part of that?"

Grayson smiled at me—a small one, but it felt good.

"You're just as much of a double-edged sword as I am," Caro said. "We position you to show Joe's a family man, but everybody remembers he was cheating on his wife when you were conceived."

"This is all bullshit. Jane has nothing to do with this. She's got a good thing going at school. You don't want to mess with that," Stick said from beside me.

It was sweet, kind of, that he was sticking up for me. Little did he know there was no room at this table for sweet.

My father looked at Stick like he was something from the bottom of his shoe. "I thought you were Caro's help? How do you even *know* Jane?"

Stick looked at me, daring me to answer my father.

"He's—"

"Irrelevant for this conversation. Stick, I know you mean well, but Jane is involved, whether she wants to be or not. This campaign—and governorship—will affect her. She might as well get used to that now, and be in on the decision-making process."

Oh, crap. I hadn't even thought beyond this governor campaign. What would it mean for me to have my father be the governor of Maryland?

There was no way a simple interview with Caro, then a summer of smiling and waving from a stage, would be the end of it.

It would only be the beginning. And somehow I just knew that Maryland wouldn't be enough.

"This is bigger, right? I mean, Maryland is just the first step," I said, looking at each of them.

None of them answered, but their faces all confirmed I

was right.

"Oh, Jesus," I whispered. "Jaybird will be back forever."

"We have to win this election first, so let's not get ahead of ourselves," Grayson said, sensing my growing agitation.

Yeah, I was starting to freak out.

I kind of liked the idea of the strategizing and the power plays, and the guessing what image people would respond to. But from the table, behind the scenes.

I had a flash of me in the future on the steps of the Capitol in DC (was that even where they swore in the president?) standing next to Betsy and Joey as my father was sworn in.

It was not an image that made me feel good.

"Okay, right. Let's keep it in perspective," I said. I rubbed my hands on my pants, finding them a bit sweaty. Stick placed his hand on mine, flat against my thigh. Much as I loved the contact, I pulled my hand away and put it on the table, taking up my pen.

Just as there was no room for sweet at the table, there was also no room for comfort.

"Caro and I will do the interview together. Appear together when needed."

They were nodding, making notes. "We'll play up the 'family comes in all shapes and sizes angle' and appeal to all those coming from nontraditional families," Grayson said. "I'll have Elliot pull the numbers on that. How many families in Maryland are nontraditional."

"Have him pull current divorce and infidelity rates in both Maryland and the US while he's at it," Caro added, and Joe nodded, typing into his laptop. "It would be good to have those numbers." She looked up, as if off into space. "You see, we're just like X percent of the people in Maryland—we've made mistakes, moved on, and are doing our best for our families." It was said in a dreamy voice, and I realized she was doing a practiced answer for a possible interview question.

"Yes. Exactly," Joe said, beaming at his ex-wife.

"It was always more of a political partnership than anything else. I don't know why I was such the bad guy for just bringing a little love into the man's life," my mother had said countless times.

She was right: Joe and Caro made great partners. But there was something in my father's eyes when he looked at Caro that I'd never seen with anyone else.

"And *our* family has grown and bonded over Caro's latest battle for her life. It has really brought home to us the importance of acceptance," Joe said in his politician's voice, answering the same nonexistent reporter that Caro had.

He kind of shook himself out of it, and they smiled at each other.

I was both fascinated and appalled. And so, so on the verge of losing it, thinking that this was my future, and half my gene pool.

The *good* half!

"I can't thank you enough for bringing Jane out here... Stick, is it?" my father said to Stick. "Getting her to bond with Caro is going to make this so much easier. It's going to look so authentic."

My body jerked. Grayson looked at Joe like he was an idiot. Caro laid her hand on mine and said, "That's because it is...authentic."

I slid my hand from underneath her cool one and looked at Stick. "Are you fucking kidding me?"

"What?" he said. His eyes were pinballing around from person to person, not getting that they'd totally outed him as part of some undercover assignment.

To use me.

TWENTY-TWO

※

"YOU KNOW, I thought I had my eyes wide open. I thought I knew exactly what to expect with those vipers in there," I said, pointing back to the dining room as I walked through the house, toward the kitchen.

All I really wanted to do was leave, but I'd wanted away from the table so badly that I'd left my stuff in the dining room and had turned toward the kitchen instead of the front door.

"I even knew Caro was capable of…befriending me for the greater good." I was in the kitchen now, the scene of all those afternoons of sharing tea with Caro. Of laughing with her over memories of her kids and my father—memories I had no right to, but wanted desperately to hear.

Desperate. The word I most conjured up when thinking of my mother.

And that thought—that I was my mother's daughter after all—sent me into a near rage. Which I directed at Stick.

I whirled on him, and he nearly ran into me. "And you," I said, sticking my finger into his chest. "How *dare* you sell me out."

I went to push at him again, but he grabbed my arm. "I don't know what the hell you're talking about. I don't know what *any* of you are talking about."

I wrenched my arm free, wanting to jab at him again, but

also wanting to be away from this place. Away from that room of political scheming, where you never knew what was sincere and what was just positioning.

"God!" I turned and walked away from Stick—further from the dining room. I looked outside to the estate grounds. What snow had fallen had now melted, and though you couldn't really call the landscape green, it was promising to be so very soon.

I went to the French doors and walked outside, the breeze cool, but not as bracing as it had been just weeks ago when I'd started coming here with Stick.

Which, apparently, was all part of some master plan.

"Unbelievable," I said as I walked across the grounds, not really caring where I went. The ground was hard in places and soft in others, the thawing process beginning.

"What is your *deal*?" Stick said as he caught up to me. He took hold of my elbow and steered me to the guesthouse where he sometimes stayed.

I tried to shake him off, but his grip tightened. Not so that it hurt, but I knew I wasn't going to be free of him.

That thought made a bark of laughter rise from me, and he looked over. "Jane? What the hell?"

We reached the guesthouse, and he opened the door and gently pushed me inside. I heard him close and lock the door behind him. "Okay," he said from behind me. "Now. What the fuck?"

I turned on him. "Are you serious? What the fuck? They totally ratted you out in there. And you're surprised that I'm pissed?"

"What? What your dad said? That I brought you here to bond with Caro so you'd be more...amenable?"

I scoffed at his nonchalant questioning of what I took as a very large betrayal. "Umm...*yeah*." My voice sounded shrill to my ears, and I realized with a blinding flash of clarity that I sounded just like my mother did when she'd yell at my father that she wanted her own Dotty.

And that realization sent me over the edge. "How *dare* you manipulate me like that. Don't you think there are enough strings being pulled around here—and for all of my fucking life, thank you very much. It would be nice to have something—*someone*—that wasn't knee deep in their shit."

He came toward me, and I backed away. I vaguely noticed the living area of the small guesthouse on one side, and a bed on the other. For all the afternoons I'd spent at Caro's house, I'd never been in here. Only the main house and the garage. There was a door behind me that must lead to the bathroom. And a small kitchen area off the living room. Small and tasteful, except for the jeans lying on the floor next to the bed, and the sweat socks piled to one side of the bedside table. The only clue that Stick had invaded this private sanctuary.

He was still following me, stalking me, and my back hit the far wall.

"You honestly believed that shit your father was spewing?"

"Yes," I said. I put my hand out to stop Stick from coming closer. He snorted disdain at the movement, took my hand and raised it over my head, pinning it against the wall.

"No you don't. You did notice that it was your father who said that, right? Not Caro or Grayson? And you get that your dad is, shall we say, not the mastermind of the group."

"All the more reason that he'd be the one to slip up and let the cat out of the bag." I knew what would happen if I reached out my other hand. He would pin that one too. And that was what I wanted. I wanted to provoke Stick. I wanted to lose control. I wanted to feel his hands on mine as they held me to the wall.

I raised my hand and pushed at his chest. We both knew

it was halfhearted, but he didn't scoff this time as he grabbed my wrist and brought it up to meet my other one, holding both in one strong hand.

"He didn't slip up. There was nothing to slip. He made the wrong conclusion."

"I don't believe you," I said.

He stepped into me, pinning me with his body as tightly as he did with my hands. "Yes you do," he whispered. He dropped his head and nuzzled my neck, his tongue making a quick graze across my jawbone. "I don't know if Caro played you, though I'd like to think she didn't." He kissed his way up my neck. I arched back, giving access, wanting more. "But I wasn't a part of any master plan. Not one that included you. I wouldn't do that."

He kissed me, and I devoured his mouth, as if I could believe his words more if I tasted from where they'd come.

Peppermint, always peppermint. I got so aroused from the scent of stupid peppermint these days.

He broke the kiss, resting his forehead on mine. "You believe me, Jane." It wasn't a question.

"I'm just trying to find one decent human being in my life, you know? One…good guy in this whole mess. Of either gender. A white hat out there in the sea of black ones," I said softly.

"You have," he said, leaning back so he could meet my eyes. "I never proclaimed to be a white hat. But in this"—he pressed his body into mine—"with us"—he tilted into me, letting his erection rock into me—"I'm a good guy. *Your* good guy. Or, at least, I want to be."

"Stick," I whispered, the futility of the situation—*our* situation—coming through in my voice.

He bristled, and I could tell I'd hurt him like I had that very first day he'd brought me Yvette. So long ago now, and yet had anything really changed?

How many times had I kissed that mouth? Tasted peppermint as our tongues swirled and danced? And every time I swore it would be the last.

But not today. Today I needed more. I needed all of Stick.

I pushed my body into his, blocking out the knowledge that there couldn't be more between us. "Do it."

He stared me down. "Do what?" He knew exactly what I meant. What I needed.

"Do it," I said again. He gave a small shake of the head. I pushed my hips deeper into him, pressed my boobs out. "Take me."

"Against a wall?"

"Seems as good a place as any," I said. His eyes were on my chest, which was moving up and down as the whole scene got me more and more excited.

"You want our first time to be up against a wall? When there's a perfectly good bed five feet away." His free hand skimmed up my body, from my waist to the side of my breast then back down and around. He slid it around and grabbed my ass, pulling me even closer into him. I mentally cursed the jeans and layers of tops that kept him from my bare skin.

"You don't get it," I said.

His eyes narrowed on mine. "What don't I get?" He rocked into me again, and I couldn't help but let out a tiny gasp. Much as we'd kissed in the past weeks, Yvette had always been chaperone against any kind of grinding action. And man, it felt good to be grinding against Stick.

"That this isn't our *first* time. It's our *only* time."

"Oh, Jane, you are so wrong about that." His hand dropped from mine and both of his palms bracketed my face, his fingers resting on my cheekbones, as he kissed me again. Harder and deeper than before. He tasted so fresh and clean. But it wasn't enough, not today, when I felt so raw, so vulnerable.

Shit, I hated being vulnerable.

I sucked on his tongue as I started clawing at his hoodie, needing it off him. Needing to see the shoulders and chest that I'd only been able to feel through cotton and coats. Sensing my urgency, he followed suit, his hands leaving my face and going to the hem of my tunic, pulling it up my body.

We had to stop kissing to remove his hoodie and my gauzy tunic. Then his long-sleeved tee and my knit henley. Finally his chest was bare, and I ran my hands down the smooth, lean, taut muscles. Until he jerked my arms up to get my tank top off me.

"Enough tops, much?" he said. I was about to throw a zinger back at him, but I was entranced by his chest and shoulders, all lean muscle and lankiness. I'd assumed he'd have tattoos, but his skin was ink-free. And a hairless chest, too, so smooth to my touch. Just a sprinkling of hair at his navel, running down past the waistband of his jeans.

My hand slid down, down, reaching for his zipper, when he put a hand at the base of my throat and gently held me against the wall. I looked up at him, but his gaze was about a foot lower than my eyes.

"Jesus Christ," he whispered as he stared at my chest. My—yes, I hated to admit it—heaving-with-excitement chest. "I thought you might be hiding something spectacular under all those funky tops. But God, Jane, it should be illegal to hide that. You're…"

"Huge?" I said.

His hands were on my breasts, pushing them up, as if taking in their weight. I had on a black bra, just a plain cotton one. The white of my skin spilled over the cups normally, and even more so as Stick molded and shaped me. Finally he moved the cups underneath each breast, lifting them up even more.

"Well, yeah, huge. But so much more than that." He bent down and took a nipple in his mouth and began sucking. My head dropped back against the wall; the sensation was so intense I wasn't sure I could keep my neck straight. "So pretty," he murmured as he moved to the other side and continued. He licked the nipple first, watching it pebble and harden, then finally took it in his mouth.

I ran my hands up his shoulders, across his neck, and held him to me, not wanting the sensation of what he was doing to me to ever end. I planted my fingers in his hair, weaving through the thick mass of waves.

I would have been happy to hold him to me like that all night, but soon he kissed his way down my stomach and dropped to his knees. "Lean back," he said, and I put my back to the wall, easing my bottom away from it, creating a bit of an angle. "Raise your hands," he said, his voice rough with arousal. Which was okay, because I was fairly certain I couldn't even speak right then.

I lifted my hands over my head, stretching them, loving how my breasts rose with me, the cups of my bra still underneath, as if framing them. Stick watched my every movement, his eyes following the rise and fall as his fingers undid my jeans' button and then fly. He slid the denim over my hips (not a small task) and down my legs. One leg at a time, I stepped out of them, and he tossed them aside.

"Take your bra off," he told me as he moved to rid me of my panties.

Not quite believing that I kind of liked him telling me what to do, I again followed his orders, and soon my bra and panties joined my other clothes on the floor. He hooked a hand under my left knee and lifted it up. Running a palm along my outer thigh, he placed my leg over his shoulder, then moved closer to me. He kissed around me. On my stomach, hips, thighs—everywhere but where I wanted his mouth most.

Needed his mouth most.

He looked up at me then and grinned, knowing he had me right where he wanted me. "Oh, just do it already," I said. He laughed, his breath still leaving him as his mouth settled right on the core of me.

My head dropped back and his mouth left my body. "Unh-uh. Watch me." When my head came back and I looked down at him, he gave a nod and tasted me again.

Oh, what a talented tongue Stick Whatever had. I knew it could tangle with me both figuratively and literally, but he still had a few tricks up his sleeve.

He licked and sucked and a finger, then two, joined in with his lips and tongue. When I didn't think I could stand it, my head would start to drop and he'd stop, causing me to quickly get back in line and watch what he was doing to my body.

"Come for me, Jane," he said, and like all his other commands, I obeyed. Shattering. Just…shattering. My hands had to have been hurting his head; I was pulling and twisting his hair as my peak just kept climbing and climbing. My body convulsed as he continued, not allowing me to come back down until he was ready.

And he wasn't ready for a long time.

When he was, he quickly got to his feet and walked the few steps to the bedside table, where he opened the drawer and pulled out a condom. He tore open the package and handed it to me, while his hands went back to my breasts, playing and twisting the nipples. It made it very hard for me to concentrate long enough to get his jeans undone, pushed down, along with his boxers, below his ass, give a few quick strokes of his hard cock and roll the condom on.

I didn't even bother pushing his jeans all the way down,

and he didn't seem to want to take the time either. As soon as the condom was on, he lifted my leg again, positioned himself at my entrance and pushed deep inside me.

I wasn't sure if his groan or mine was louder. He stretched me and filled me, and at first it felt like too much. And then it felt…right. Not a word I conjured up when thinking about Stick and me together. But yeah, it was right. We…fit.

He leaned into me, then picked up my other leg, both off the ground now, my back at an angle against the wall, his body leveraging mine. I wrapped my arms around his shoulders and hung on. I was splayed open, totally trusting in Stick to hold me up. To take care of me. It was an odd sensation, but as his movements inside me picked up pace, I relaxed and caught his rhythm.

He sensed it right away. Of course he did. I both hated and loved that. "That's it," he said in my ear, his face against mine, our deep breaths matched. "Open that awesome body to me, Jane. Let me all the way in."

I shifted a tiny bit in his arms, and we both sighed at the exquisite slide that brought him even closer, deeper.

"Yes," I said, not able to help myself. "Yes, right there." He knew he'd found the spot, and picked up his pace, his fingers pressing into the backs of my thighs as he drove harder into me, slamming me against the wall with each stroke.

Just before his release, he bit my earlobe, and that, coupled with his hard strokes, sent me over the edge again. My whole body shuddered, and I felt the spasms rocket through his body as I held on to him.

He pumped a few more strokes as I came down from my high, then he rested his face in the crook of my neck. His body leaned in to mine, stretching me even further, and I gasped his name, feeling the aftershocks.

We stayed like that—our bodies joined, with my feet

still off the ground, Stick's strong arms holding my—not insignificant—weight.

I don't know how long it was before he turned around, sliding me further onto his body as I left the wall. He carried me the few steps to the bed and grabbed the bedding with one hand, giving it a yank down so that he could lay me down on the sheets. He followed me down, still staying inside me.

I tucked my head into his chest, placing a soft kiss on his pec, not wanting to look at him. Not wanting him to know he'd just completely destroyed me.

As no other man ever had.

TWENTY-THREE

Stick

I ruled the road. And then I was sideswiped by Jane.

I LEFT THE BED. Left Jane dozing under the sheet. A shame to cover her luscious body, but when the sweat that we'd worked up cooled down, she'd be chilled.

I shook my head as I walked to the bathroom, unbelieving that I was thinking shit about how a girl I'd just banged might get chilled.

Except she wasn't just any girl. And it wasn't your regular old bang.

It was Jane. And it was…unfuckingbelievable.

The sun was nearly down and the guesthouse was dim. We hadn't turned on any lights when I'd dragged Jane here. There hadn't been time. I'd had her pinned against the wall too quickly.

And then she'd ground against me and all logical thought had left me. Instinct—and desperately wanting Jane naked for months—had taken hold.

And then I'd taken hold of her.

I switched on the light in the bathroom and shut the door so the glare wouldn't rouse her.

I didn't think she was asleep, just in more of a post-sex haze. And I was too, but I wanted to get rid of the condom and clean up a little so we could commence with round two.

I peeled the rubber off, then stopped. Something looked a little different. It'd been a while since I'd had sex (since before that first kiss with Jane when I'd dropped off Yvette), but I knew what a used rubber looked like. Not that I scientifically studied them or anything, but if you see what looks like blood on anything, you take a closer look.

I held the thing together at the top, then ran it under the tap so water would run off the outside of it. And the water turned pink in the basin. Yeah, blood.

She could have been having her period, though she hadn't brought it up and I hadn't seen anything to make me think she was.

Or she could have *just* started her period.

But no. I knew. Jane had been a virgin until about an hour ago.

I wrapped the condom in a couple of Kleenex (Dotty didn't need to be dealing with the sight of that) and put it in the trash. I washed up and took a wet washcloth and dry towel back to the bedroom with me.

"Hey," Jane said as I sat down on my side of the bed. My side. Like we had "sides" already. Like I hadn't been sprawled right in the center of this lush bed the nights I'd stayed here.

But yeah, I'd take a side for sure if it meant sharing my bed with Jane.

She had her back to me, lying on her side, the line of her curves playing like the most erotic roller coaster ever.

"Hey," I said. I laid the warm, wet washcloth on her bared shoulder, and draped the towel over her hip, on top of the sheet.

She reached up and pulled the washcloth in front of her. "Thanks," she said, and the hand and the cloth disappeared under the sheet.

God, I wanted to be the one to push that warm heat against her tender flesh. But I let her do it. Losing your virginity against a wall in a bout of emotional—okay, angry—sex might have been more than any girl could handle in one day without the guy pawing at her afterward because he just couldn't get enough of her.

But again, this wasn't any girl. And my guess was that Jane could handle just about anything.

"Why'd you pick out a Corvette?" she asked. She put the used washcloth on the floor on the other side of the bed. The towel was next to disappear under the sheet. The movements she made drove me crazy with want, and I slipped under the sheet and pulled the duvet (or whatever Dotty had called it) up to cover my newly burgeoning woody.

It didn't work; Jane's eye went right to it when she rolled over onto her back and looked over at me. A brow quirked, but she didn't remark on it. Just repeated her question, which I'd been too horned up about the thought of her under that sheet to answer. "Why'd you pick out a Corvette?"

"What do you mean?"

"You picked it out, right?"

I tried to remember what I'd said that first day, and if I was giving anything away by telling her how it had gone down.

"It's okay. I know you would have done it. Grayson wouldn't want to be bothered with choosing a model—beyond saying it had to be American-made. And my father... My father just wouldn't have given a shit."

Yep, that was pretty much exactly how it had gone down.

"You picked it out, right?"

"Yes," I said. I reached out and laid a hand on her hip. The towel was underneath her mostly, but part of it was lying over her hip, and a bit of her stomach.

Caro had nothing but the best of everything—including in her little-used guesthouse—and the towels were big, fluffy and soft, but they felt like burlap next to Jane's smooth skin.

I rolled onto my side to face her, keeping my hand gently on her, as if I didn't want to scare her off.

She stayed where she was, on her back, looking up at the ceiling. I'd left the light on in the bathroom and the door about halfway open. The beam of light cut across our bodies around waist level. I raised the duvet up higher on her side, letting it rest just under her breasts.

Those babies should never—*ever*—be covered up at all, but I could deal with the sheet. When she'd breathe, the sheet would rise and fall on those sweet tits with just a hint of her nipples jutting against the white, crazy-high-thread-count cotton.

Nothing had ever tasted sweeter than having them in my mouth.

"Stop staring at my boobs and answer the question," she said, though her eyes were closed.

I smiled, maybe because she couldn't see it. "You're a Corvette, Jane, all the way."

She stilled for just a second before a grin crossed her face. "You mean because I've got great curves and am fast?"

"No, though you've got great curves." I moved closer, and my hand edged up her body, off the towel completely (thank God) and over those great curves. I cupped one of her tits in my hand and flicked my thumb across the nipple, it already pebbling and hardening at my touch.

"And I'd hardly say fast. It's been eight weeks. Twelve since Betsy's wedding."

She didn't ask eight weeks since what. She knew it was that day with Yvette. The day she'd sat in front of this huge place and told me about coming there as a kid with her mother.

The day she'd pissed me off and I'd kissed her senseless.

Well, that actually could have been any day in the past eight weeks.

"You're a Corvette because you announce your presence. In some ways you want people to notice you." I thought of the funky clothes she wore, so different from what Lily and the Bribury Basics wore. Jane never wanted to blend in, and yet… "You don't want to announce everything about yourself. *You* want to define yourself. Not let somebody else do it."

"And Yvette does that?"

"Yes."

She waved a hand in dismissal. At least, I thought it was dismissal. My mind was thinking about how great it felt when she moved with my hand cupping her. I squeezed her and brushed my thumb against her nipple again, and she squelched a moan, I supposed not wanting me to know how much she liked it. But she did press her thighs together, the sight of which made my dick all the harder.

"How do you figure I define myself? I've been nothing but a pawn my whole life. If that debacle in there today proved nothing else, it proved that."

I pulled my mind away from how great her tits felt and tried to get it right, feeling like I *had* to get it right. Not so I could keep feeling her up (and hopefully get her hands on me, too), but because I could sense something in her. I wouldn't go as far as to say she was vulnerable, but…a shield was down. Not down very far, and surely not down for long. But I knew it was my chance to take a shot.

"That's the thing. You *know* you've been a pawn in other people's games, but you refuse to play. You're trying to make the rules bend to your advantage."

"That's just playing their game, learning what they've taught me by example."

"Maybe. But maybe you've got everyone fooled and we'll all be playing by your rules."

"Ha, I've got no one fooled."

My hand slid down, regretfully leaving her soft breast, and I rested it on her belly, just above her mound. "You don't think everyone is fooled about you not being a virgin?"

Everything about her stilled. I brushed my hand gently from hipbone to hipbone, not saying a word.

"Well, of course you figured it out. You've probably been with tons of virgins."

"Fewer than you'd think," I said, which was the truth. In my neighborhood, girls didn't stay virginal very long once they'd hit puberty.

"Are you okay?" I asked.

She nodded, but didn't look over at me. I sat up a little, resting my head on my hand, my elbow on the bed, looking down at her.

"You want to talk about it?" Words I'd probably never in my life said to a girl before. Yet they rolled off my tongue pretty easily. I wanted to hear Jane's story.

"God, no," she said. She moved to cover her face with a hand, but I took it in mine and returned our clasped hands back under the covers to rest on her hipbone, her palm flat on her skin, mine on hers.

"Why the big talk about wanting to bang the prof? Talking about slut-shaming you, and that you'd been with other guys?"

She shrugged, and I watched as the sheet edged a tiny bit lower. "I never actually *said* I'd been with anyone."

I thought back. She was right. "No, you didn't. But you certainly implied that you…had more experience than you obviously have."

"It's nobody's business who I have or haven't slept with."

"You're absolutely right, it's not. But why the misdirection?

Why not just say nothing?"

She turned her head away from me, and I thought that maybe she was putting the shield back in place. I squeezed her hand, but didn't say anything else.

She turned her head back, but continued to look up, not at me. "You know that incident with Edgar Prescott?"

"Who?"

"That old guy at Betsy's wedding?"

My body tensed just thinking about that old perv's hands on Jane. "Yeah?"

"Stuff like that's been happening since I turned thirteen and grew these," she said, bobbing her chin in the general direction of her tits.

She had a stellar body—tall, but all curves. Though you wouldn't know it with the goofy, baggy clothes she wore.

Ah…that was why the baggy clothes.

"Boys my age I could handle. I put them in their place."

I smiled down at her. "I'll just bet you did."

"But there were a lot of Edgar Prescotts. Men who knew my story, knew my mother's history. Men who assumed the apple didn't fall far from the slut tree."

I tensed again. I knew she would have handled Prescott if I hadn't gotten to them. But had there been others, when she was younger, that she hadn't been able to handle?

"It never went too far, and most stepped back with a few good verbal shots." And I'd just bet she shot some good ones. "But a rumor started at boarding school about a teacher and me. And I just kind of let it go. I was tired of it all by then. Tired of denying the lies. So I just let it hang out there." She shrugged. "I never said anything ever happened when it didn't, but I never said it didn't, either. By the time I got to Bribury I was kind of used to the sexual swagger."

"It's just part of the shield," I said, not really intending to say it out loud.

I thought she'd bristle, and when she moved, I knew she was going to turn away from me, get out of bed. I didn't even want to examine how much the thought of that killed me.

But she didn't leave. She turned to her side, facing me. She untangled our hands and put hers under her head, her palm resting along her cheek. Her other hand moved to take mine, and she placed them both back on her hip. And I swear to God, my breath hitched and caught just looking at her as she watched me.

"I don't like how much you get me," she said quietly.

"I know," I whispered, my eyes on her lips, still a little puffy from the angry kisses against the wall.

"I get you, too," she said, her mouth now inches from mine.

"I know," I said, and bent my head the few inches to kiss her.

I DROVE BACK to Bribury that night, Jane wanting to sit in the passenger seat.

We'd gone two more times, and each time it just got better, though I would have sworn that was impossible. But I was learning her body, much like you learned a new car. And, better yet, she was learning mine.

Yeah, I taught her well how to handle a stick. And with more than just her hand.

It was midnight by the time I'd gone back into the house to get Jane's and my stuff. The house was dark except for the under-counter lights in the kitchen, left on by Dotty so I could see.

I peeked in on Caroline and made sure she was okay. She was deep in sleep with the monitor on so Dotty would be able to hear her if she needed anything. I had one for the guesthouse, too, on nights I stayed. Which were now more and more frequent.

Jane met me around the front of the house—said she didn't want to go in in case Caro was still up. "She'll know what we've been doing," she said, and a cute little blush crept up her cheeks.

Honestly, I didn't think Jane was capable of blushing.

Jane sat beside me in the car, reclined a bit, her eyes closed. Presumably putting her shield back in place. I drove with my hand high on her thigh except when I had to shift. I expected her to brush it off, but she didn't.

We drove in silence and I thought about the past twelve weeks since Betsy's wedding. And even the events that brought me to the wedding.

Brought me to Jane.

I'd been summoned to go to the wedding by Spaulding. About a week earlier he'd made me an offer I couldn't refuse (and yeah, it had felt a little Godfatherish at the time), but it would be contingent on Caro's approval. I'd lain pretty low at the reception, blending in as only a thief knew how to do, until I saw Jane. More significantly, Jane in that dress.

She'd been a total ball buster the few times I'd been around her when she'd been with Lily. But there was just something about her that stayed with me.

I didn't want to be drawn to her—especially after I found out who she was. And I knew she didn't want to be drawn to me, either. I could tell she thought I was nothing but a douchebag criminal who was weighing down her best friend's boyfriend.

She wasn't wrong. But she didn't *really* know me.

But now? Yeah, I kind of thought that she did. About as much as I was getting to know the real her.

The shield made it tough. And there were days when I

didn't even want to bother trying to get through it. She was a lot of work, Jane. And I wasn't even sure it was worth it.

Until today. Being inside her. All that energy—anger, fear, but also determination. She was just…fierce. I didn't doubt for one minute that if she ever harnessed it all, she could rule the world.

And she wouldn't be able to do that with an ex-car-thief by her side.

She knew it. Knew it from the beginning, even before I grasped it, before I'd even really thought about her and me. And it had royally pissed me off.

Not that I was looking for a life partner at twenty-one or anything. Shit no. I loved the freedom I had—needed it in my line of work.

My *previous* line of work.

I had a couple of very loose, very casual "friends with benefits" situations here and there, mostly with women in my "network" who were just as happy as I to keep it no strings attached.

But even that, casual as it was, I put an end to after that first day I'd kissed Jane. I'd known even then something was going to happen with Jane, something I didn't want or deserve. Something I fought every time since that day I'd brought her Yvette.

Yvette. Christ, Jane was the most original girl I'd met, and she couldn't have come up with something better for a Corvette than Yvette?

I must have grunted my amusement, because Jane turned out of her fog and softly said, "What?"

I liked the fierce Jane. The Jane that gave as good as she got. Hell, gave a *ton* better than she got. The Jane who took none of my shit and called me on it every time.

But this Jane? Highlighted by the glow of the dash, leaning

back, her hair tousled and eyes still just a tiny bit dazed.

This Jane made me forget that it was a very bad idea for us to be anything more than fuck buddies.

Because...I wanted so much more.

"Nothing," I said. "Just thinking."

She smiled at me, and my memory raced to just a while ago when she'd smiled at me before taking me in that sweet (and yet tart) mouth.

"First time for everything," she said, with no real bite. The smile stayed with her as she turned her head back to the road.

I would have to move very slowly with Jane. Not that eight weeks from first kiss (*real* kiss; I didn't count that bullshit on the dance floor) to falling into bed wasn't excruciatingly slow.

Not that I hadn't gone home and jerked off thinking about what might have been every time I drove away from her in Lot H.

A parking lot I was now pulling into. Funny, most days with Jane I couldn't wait to get to Lot H, knowing that even though I told myself I wasn't going to reach for her, I would. And even though she'd probably told herself over and over not to do it, she'd reach for me, too.

I fucking loved driving into Lot H with Jane. Except tonight, there was no way it could get any better in Lot H than it had for the past five or six hours in Caro's guesthouse.

And though I was willing to give Yvette's console another workout, Jane looked beat. Well, yeah, having a major sexfest your first time out would do that to you.

"Wait here," I said to her when I pulled the Vette alongside my car. "I'll heat mine up and then drive you back to the dorm."

I thought she'd probably balk at that, saying she could walk, not wanting to be seen being dropped off in front of her dorm at nearly one in the morning by a thug in an old Dodge

Charger. A supremely restored, mint, cherry-red Charger, but still.

"Thanks," she said, and I had a glimmer of hope that maybe if I kept Jane well satisfied that I had a chance of keeping her close.

It was time to come clean with myself at least, and admit that that was exactly what I wanted. Jane. Close. For a long time.

Even though the days were getting warmer, it was still cold as shit when I got out and went to my car. I turned the heater on full blast and looked out my window to Jane right next to me in the passenger side of Yvette.

She turned and just stared at me, her face stark, no emotion showing, as she studied me.

Shit, it was the exact look she had on her face that first day. One that I had correctly read as her realizing she was too good for me and there could never be anything between us.

It had pissed me off that day.

Today, it would kill me.

I waited, not looking away from her, dying inside, but determined not to show it. Any second now she'd get this pained look and then a tiny bit of pity, then look away.

But it didn't come. Instead, a small smile crossed her cute face, then blossomed into a full-blown grin. Then she—yes, Jane!—blew me a kiss.

And I took the first full breath of relief since the first time I kissed her.

I waved her over, and as she made her way, I once again thought, and even said out loud to the empty car, "Who are you, Jane Winters?"

TWENTY-FOUR

❖

Jane

IT WASN'T LIKE I was saving my virginity for my wedding night or anything. And beyond all my big talk, I wanted to… *crave* the guy who would be my first. I'd just never found anyone I wanted to tear my clothes off with.

Until Stick. And that day, up against the wall? The tearing of clothes couldn't come quickly enough.

So, yeah, I was no longer a virgin. And in the next week and a half, we stamped out any remaining doubt.

It wasn't that I was necessarily holding out for Prince Charming the past few years. Let's face it, Stick was nobody's idea of Prince Charming. And of course I'd had opportunities. But I'd never been that tempted.

Before Stick. So, maybe he was *my* Prince Charming.

The goodbyes in Lot H were more bittersweet now—a parting after an exhausting afternoon/evening of very good sex.

At least, I thought it was good. I didn't have a lot to compare it to, but Stick seemed to suggest by his groans and occasional "hell yeah"s and "that's so fucking amazing"s that we were on the right track.

It wasn't every day, and it wasn't every time we went to Caro's, but it was nearly that.

I went to the health clinic and got on the pill, but we still faithfully used condoms each time. I was stretching it enough by sleeping with a car thief townie, I wasn't about to pull a Bristol Palin and walk across the campaign stage totally knocked up.

Two weeks after our first time together, Stick called and said we were going to go to dinner with Lily and Lucas, not out to Caro's, and to maybe dress up a bit.

"You mean like a double date?" I said, stunned. I still hadn't mentioned anything to Lily about Stick and me... being Stick and me. I had told her about my visits to Caro's, and mentioned that she was not doing well. Lily was Grayson Spaulding's daughter and could be trusted to keep that secret.

"Yeah, like a double date. I guess," Stick said.

"Why?"

He let out that exasperated sigh that he sometimes gave me—usually right before he kissed me silly. "Because that's what couples do."

"We're a couple?" I said without really thinking about it. I mean, yeah, we were sleeping together. At Bribury that didn't mean much. And in theory I was on board with the casual sex thing, the meaningless hookups. But then, why had I still been a virgin before Stick?

"We're not?" Attitude in his voice now. Understandable, but we'd never had any kind of "talk" about us. No talk of exclusivity or anything like that.

Not that any other guy interested me now that I knew what Stick could do to my body.

"I guess," I said, with not much conviction.

"Jesus, Jane," he said.

"What time should I be at Lot H?" I said quickly, trying to switch gears before he got pissed. Although a pissed-off Stick was a sexy-as-hell Stick.

Another sigh. "Not Lot H. I'll pick you up out front. We'll take my car so we all fit."

"Seriously. Like, this is for real? A 'pick you up, dinner with our friends' double date?"

"Yes, Jane. Like a real date. A real double date."

"And Lily and Lucas already know?"

"Yep. So you got out of having to tell your roomie you're sleeping with me. Lucas already told her."

"How do you know I didn't?"

"Did you?" Silence, then a small snort from him. "Yeah, I didn't think so."

A sigh from me. "What time, asshole?"

"Six. See you out front then. A dress would be nice."

"I don't do dresses."

"Do one tonight." Before I could argue, he disconnected. Right as Lily walked in.

As we got ready for our—still so weird to think about—double date, I brought Lily up to speed. I was careful to downplay it, but she was staring at me pretty closely.

"So…you're…"

"Sleeping together?" I finished for her. "Yes. A couple of weeks now. Really, it's no big deal. Just casual hookups. Convenient, really, because of the whole Caro thing. We've both been spending so much time out there, who would I even get a chance to sleep with?"

She studied me, then shook her head and continued to apply her makeup as we shared the mirror in the bathroom. "That part is weird, too—Stick being a caregiver to Caroline Stratton."

"It's all weird. I'm just trying to…" I didn't finish my thought, wasn't really sure how to. *Not fall in love with him? Keep my father happy? Give some peace to a woman I respect?*

"What?" Lily asked, leaning close to the mirror to put on

her mascara.

I was straightening my hair, something I hadn't done in a long time, probably since fall semester. I hated that I was actually primping for this thing. And I *really* hated that I had asked to borrow a dress from Lily.

I had a couple of my own, but they were funky, retro, gauzy things I'd picked up at a flea market in Baltimore last summer.

Tonight I wanted…armor, I guess. And looking like every other girl at Bribury was just what I needed.

When I didn't answer Lily, she didn't push. And she didn't ask any more questions, just quietly finished getting ready, leaving the bathroom before me.

When I came out, a knit, wrap-style dress in a deep jade green was lying across my bed, with pumps placed beside it.

"Thanks," I said, and she smiled at me, then started dressing. She was wearing a version of a Little Black Dress that hung on her lean, lithe body like the designer had intended.

Lily and I were the same height, same shoe size and, in some ways, the same clothing size. But where she was long and lean, toned from her swimming, I was curvy and lush (Stick's word—I'm usually not as kind). The green dress technically fit, but it was *much* more body hugging than I typically wore.

"Wow," Lily said when I zipped up the dress and stepped into the heels. "You look amazing."

I waved her compliment away, then remembered Caro chastising me about taking a compliment during one of our many talks. "Thank you," I said, smoothing my hands over my full hips, liking the feel of the material. "So do you," I added. It was true. Lily was a beautiful girl. The simplicity of her black sheath, with her hair up and simple pearl post earrings—very striking.

She checked the time on her phone. "Ready?" she asked.

"I guess," I said.

She smiled at me. "God, Jane, it's just a dinner date, not a firing squad."

"I know," I said. And really, I wasn't sure why I had this feeling of...*dread* about the whole evening.

As we rode the elevator down, it hit me. With Lily and Lucas in the know, with us going out to a public restaurant on an actual date... It was *real* with Stick now.

No more only the two of us (and Caro and Dotty—they had to know what we were doing in the guesthouse...and the garage...and against the wall of the main house on our way to the guesthouse).

It wasn't just our own little cocoon, snug as Yvette's cockpit.

It was...out there. It was real.

And I wasn't sure how I felt about that.

Though I felt a lot better when I watched Stick's reaction when I walked out of the dorm.

"Jesus Christ," he whispered as he came forward and took my hand. (Took my hand! In front of the dorm, where my fellow students were coming in and out of!)

"You look..." He looked me up and down as we walked to the car. I vaguely saw Lucas do the same with Lily, getting her into the back seat, then joining her and putting the seat back in place. Stick held the door for me as I got in, then softly shut it and crossed to the driver's side. As he crossed the front of the car he watched me through the windshield, and my body heated with the look he gave me.

Like he loved me in this dress, but couldn't wait to get me out of it.

I felt the same way.

And he looked pretty damn good, too. In a smart grey suit, crisp white shirt and black tie. His hair was slicked back, showing off his strong face.

We all made small talk as we drove to Chesney, where apparently we had a reservation at some fancy restaurant.

It was all familiar, yet kind of unreal. Lucas and Lily cuddled together in the back seat, his arm around her, she tucked into his big torso. It was Friday night, one of the nights that Lucas didn't have to work.

Stick had his hand on my thigh, slowly edging up the hem of my dress until I put my hand over his, halting his progress. He shot me a "come on" look, but I shook my head at him.

He must have told Lucas—and Lily, by extension—not to question us too much about our…relationship, because they didn't. If it had been me, I'd have been giving them the third degree.

But then, I'm not Lily. And Stick and I were definitely not Lucas and Lily.

They had an ease about them, really had right from the start. Whereas with Stick it always felt like…work. Good work, challenging work. And definitely with the satisfaction of a job well done. Or at least that was how I felt after we had sex.

But I had this twinge watching the couple in the back seat, knowing that would never be Stick and me. Maybe not me with any guy. I just couldn't imagine myself ever being that comfortable with anybody.

"We're a little early for the reservation," Stick said as we drove into Chesney. "I didn't know if you guys would be ready on time or not."

"Why wouldn't we?" I asked. "What? You think we spent hours agonizing over what dress to wear? Please." I didn't dare look at Lily in the rearview, because I knew she'd give it away that Stick's guess wasn't that far from the truth.

He shrugged. "I don't know. This is all kind of new to me, you know." He looked a little embarrassed, so I let him off the hook.

"So, yeah, we're a little early. And I have to drop something off for Caro anyway. Do you guys mind if we do that first?"

There were shrugs and "whatever"s from all three of us, and Stick drove through town and toward Chesney Hills.

When we entered Caro's estate, Stick said to me, "You know, she'd probably love to see you in that dress. Why don't you go in with me while I drop these meds off." He pointed at the small white bag in the middle of the seat.

I was about to say no when, out of the corner of my eye, I saw Lucas give Lily a meaningful look and decided I did not want to be alone in the car with the lovebirds no matter how short Stick's errand would be.

We walked into the house (Stick never knocked or rang the bell anymore), and when he called out, Caro's voice directed us to the living room.

He took my hand, which was weird, and led me down the hall. Just as we were about to turn and enter the room, I heard noise from behind me and saw that Lily and Lucas had come in the house.

I didn't know how Caro would react to strangers seeing her, so I shooed at them to go away.

"It's fine," Stick whispered, then pulled me with him as we turned into the living room.

"Surprise!" shouted a small gathering in the living room. Besides Dotty and Caro (dressed in elegant slacks and sweater set, not her normal tracksuit), there was my father and Grayson Spaulding and a woman I recognized from pictures as Lily's mother. Syd was there too, looking great in a red dress, but also looking a little uncomfortable.

Another guy was there, and he seemed to be filming me on his phone.

"What the fu—"

"Happy birthday, Jane," Caro said, stepping forward, her hand reaching out to me.

I felt Stick's hand untwine from mine, after a gentle squeeze, and it went to the small of my back. He didn't push me, just kept his hand there. Afraid I might bolt?

Lily and Lucas came up from behind us. "Were you surprised?" Lily asked, a big smile on her face. "That was the one part I didn't like of this whole plan—that we weren't already in here and could see your face when they yelled surprise."

"I was surprised," I said, my voice flat.

Lily and Lucas stepped past Stick and me and into the room. Lily going to her parents, hugging them. Her mother kissing Lucas on the cheek and Grayson shaking his hand.

Caro still stood in the center of the room, waiting for me, though her hand had dropped. My father moved to stand next to her, placing his hand at her back, much like Stick had done with me.

I bristled at the thought that Stick and I were—in any way—like my father and Caro. Stick, feeling my tension, bent and whispered in my ear.

"Shit. Did we fuck up? Say the word and we're out of here. Let them eat the damn cake by themselves."

And that was what gave me the strength to smile and enter the room, embraced by my father and his ex-wife.

Stick had my back.

TWENTY-FIVE

❖

Stick

SHIT. SHE HATED THIS. With a passion. It was obvious, at least to me. And to Lily too, judging by the concerned look she gave Jane about a half-hour into the party. Then Lily looked over at me, seeing if I was aware.

I nodded at her that I was, and that seemed to be enough for Lily, who went back to putting food on a plate from the huge buffet that someone had laid out in the dining room. Caterers probably, as it seemed too much to have come just from Dotty. And the birthday cake was definitely from a bakery—it looked like a miniature wedding cake, for Christ's sake.

It was lovely and tasteful…and it seemed like Jane hated it.

I got that maybe the shock of the surprise, and the surrounding subterfuge, would have thrown her off her game, but now, a couple of hours in, she still hadn't warmed up to the idea that these people were here to help her celebrate turning nineteen.

Elliot Somethingorother was walking around with his phone taking pictures and shooting video. He'd been there other times when I had, taking meetings with Caro about the campaign. I didn't think he'd been here when Jane had been, and I could tell that she was uncomfortable around him. Or uncomfortable with him taking pictures of the whole thing.

I mostly hung with Syd—the third roommate Jane had spoken about, but whom I'd never met. She was cool, and seemed to get how uncomfortable Jane was with it all.

"You know," she said to me as we sat in the living room, plates from the buffet balanced on our laps, "Jane never even mentioned that it was her birthday today. And I don't mean just today. Most people will say stuff like 'my birthday's coming up' or 'when I turn nineteen in a couple of weeks' or something like that. Nothing from Jane. If Grayson hadn't mentioned it to Lily, and then planned this party, we would never have known. Don't you find that weird?"

For most college kids, yes. But not Jane. Well, yeah, I found it weird even for Jane, but the fact that Jane did stuff out of the norm no longer surprised me.

"I mean," Syd continued, "obviously Jane's good at keeping secrets." She looked pointedly at me—the biggest secret Jane was keeping. *Had* been keeping. "But why bother hiding your birthday?"

"Maybe she didn't want any fuss?" I said as I watched Jane. She'd gotten a plate from the buffet and had come back into the living room with it. When her eyes found Syd and me, I motioned with my head to the empty seat beside me on the couch. And then (God, I hated to admit it) held my breath until she gave a small nod and moved toward me.

Man, she was a knockout in that green dress. The way it hugged her curves, outlined her gorgeous bust and hips, which were all swaying slightly with every step she took. The dress brought out her green eyes, and her straightened hair was sleek and stylish.

And…hot as she was, it wasn't the Jane I knew. The Jane I craved. Though I sure craved getting her alone and peeling that tight dress down and over all that body.

"Ya perv," Jane said as she got to the couch and sat beside me. "You were looking at me like Edgar Prescott did when I was wearing that bridesmaid's dress."

The comparison stung, but there was no bite in her voice. "But there's a difference," I said.

"Yeah? What?"

I leaned closer to her so Syd, on a chair across from us, wouldn't hear. "You *want* my hands all over you."

I waited for her comeback. I loved how I waited for Jane's comebacks—would it be funny, would it be lethal, would it total eviscerate me?

She looked me up and down, much like I'd just done to her as she walked over to me.

"You'd be right about that," she said. Yeah, totally eviscerated me—but in a good way this time.

Before I could come up with a way to snatch her away from this party and get her to the guesthouse, where I could slowly peel that clingy green material down and off her body, she turned to Syd and said, "So, how'd you get roped into this? And sorry, by the way, that you did."

"Do you not want me here?" There was a chip on Syd's shoulder that I recognized right away. Because I had one too.

"I don't want anyone here," Jane said. "I mean, I don't want anyone to *have* to be here." She took a bite of something from her plate, watching Syd as she chewed.

One day when we were in the garage while I was working on the cars, Jane had told me that she and Syd were sometimes oil and water. Jane had been sitting on top of the long counter that ran the length of the huge building, swinging those long legs, crossed at the ankles.

It was before we'd started having sex, and as she explained her sometimes complicated, but right now good, relationship with her third roommate, all I could think about was stepping closer and unlinking her ankles and wrapping those legs around my hips.

So, yeah, I didn't get all the nuances of what she'd said.

But now, Syd seemed to accept Jane's explanation and visibly relaxed, taking a few bites from her own plate.

"Why didn't you tell us it was your birthday?" Syd asked Jane.

I felt her shrug next to me. "I've hated my birthday since I was ten. Honestly—and this is the truth—I kind of block it out. So, yeah, it was *really* a surprise."

"So, you didn't think something was up because of the double date and asking you to wear a dress?" I said.

"Asking me? More like telling me. And no, I didn't even put it together that it could be birthday related. Because I didn't think any of you knew it was my b-day."

"Caro knew. She's the one that got it all rolling, I guess," Syd said.

Jane seemed to stiffen for a second, then relaxed. But I noticed she'd stopped eating. "Yes, Caro would know my birthday. When I was a little kid, she'd drag Joey and Betsy to some hotel—or at least a neutral site—and make them give me gifts and wish me happy birthday. They hated it. I hated it. But it was important to her that her kids knew me, even if it was for only one day a year."

I held my plate with one hand and put the other at the small of Jane's back. But she leaned forward, away from my touch, not wanting comfort. Not wanting to seem weak.

The move would probably piss off most guys, but it just made me…like Jane all the more.

Yeah, I was *way* beyond "like" with Jane. But, just as she'd moved away from my touch, I mentally moved away from that thought—that there was more than just a grudging mutual respect, and hot-hot-hot sex between me and Jane Winters.

"What? You think I'm going to pull out the violins and play for your sad story?" Syd said to Jane. "At least you had presents on your birthday—and from rich kids, no less."

A moment passed where the two girls just stared at each other and I kept my mouth shut. Then Jane cracked a smile. "Bitch," she said to Syd with no malice in her voice, almost as a tip of the cap.

"Takes one to know one," Syd said easily, and the two of them smiled at each other.

We all ate in silence. The food—no surprise—was first rate, and I gobbled up my full plate.

"What I don't get," Jane said after a while, "was how Caro felt comfortable enough to have Syd and Lily and Lucas here. Seeing her in her condition."

"What do you mean? I'm not going to say anything," Syd said, the chip back firmly on her shoulder.

Jane waved a hand. "*I* know that. I can vouch for you and Lily. And I'm sure Stick vouched for Lucas. But if I were Caro and didn't want news of how sick I was getting out, I wouldn't take any chances."

"It won't matter soon," Caro said from behind us. I started to get up, but she motioned me to stay seated so I did. She made her way around the couch and sat in the other chair, beside Syd and facing Jane and me, in the small seating area tucked away to one side of the mammoth living room.

"What do you mean?" Jane said. I could hear the fear in her voice. Did Caro mean she didn't have much longer?

We'd talked about it a lot, and Caro still wouldn't let me call Betsy or Joey and get them back here. Based on her physical abilities, and what I'd seen my father go through at the end, I would guess Caro still had several weeks left.

Not that I was any kind of expert or anything, but I'd

done a lot of reading about it all when my dad was dying, and even more now that I was the primary caregiver to Caro.

I put my hand at Jane's back again, and this time she leaned into it—wanting the comfort now. Needing it to hear what Caro would say.

But it wasn't a death sentence Caro was handing down. At least not hers.

"We have the interview scheduled. You, Joe and I will be meeting with Amanda Teller on Monday to do the family interview. There will be no way around news of my condition getting out after that. We'll try to control that, but…"

One would think that Jane would relax at that news—that it wasn't that Caro only had days to live. But no, Jane tensed up even more.

Because in a few days Jane would have to endorse her father and pretend they were all one big happy family.

Sure enough, even as I rubbed it, her back went ramrod straight.

TWENTY-SIX

❖

Jane

THE REST OF THE PARTY went by in a blur. There were presents, which were excruciating to sit through. Not that I didn't like stuff, but it all reminded me of those birthdays years ago. I half expected to hear my mother screaming from the next room that it was time for Caro to leave, that Pandora was my mother, all while my father tried to placate her and Caro would sit with a serene smile etched on her face.

But my mother wasn't in the next room, and Stick sat next to me while the whole thing was going on, giving me a sense of calm about the whole night.

Yeah, Stick was my calming influence—how's that for an oxymoron?

My father and Caro gave me an all-expenses paid trip to New York for a weekend for myself, Lily and Syd. Included were huge gift certificates for Barneys and a very fancy spa and salon.

It was very generous, and very nice of them to include Lily and Syd. But I knew the advantage to them was a. making sure I went (by including my pals), and b. ensuring I'd have nice, *appropriate* clothes to wear this summer while out campaigning (Barneys). There would be no thrift store shopping on this trip.

Lily and Lucas got me a monogrammed keychain, which was very nice, and I knew Yvette's key fob would be going on it soon. Syd gave me a really nice leather-bound journal. "For your adventures this summer," she said. The Spauldings gave me gift cards to several of the restaurants in Schoolport.

And Stick gave me a pair of sunglasses and a scarf. It wasn't the big, dramatic, drapey kind of scarf that Syd had gotten and which I thought was cool. It was smaller, lighter, in a pretty green with a small pattern of gold woven through it.

"It's to wear when you're driving the Vette, now that the weather is near top-down level. Like some French aristocrat or something, driving across the countryside."

I didn't know what movies he'd been watching, but it was perfect, and I told him so. There was an awkward moment when I could tell he wanted to kiss me, but wouldn't with so many people around. Which was fine with me—I didn't need any big PDA either.

We were saved by Dotty, who brought in the cake, candles lit and all. They sang for me and I blew out the candles.

"Did you make a wish?" Syd asked.

I looked at Stick. "I wish I knew your real, full name."

Everyone laughed. Stick just smiled and said, "It doesn't come true if you tell people what you wished for."

I looked over at Lucas, brow raised. "I don't rat out friends," he said, his hands in the air.

The night went on, cake was eaten, small talk was made. Those of us under twenty-five naturally congregated together, as did Caro, Joe, the Spauldings and Elliot. From the bored look on Lily's mom's face, I guessed they were talking about Joe's campaign. She was the only one in the group that looked bored.

Everyone left around ten. Lucas took Stick's car and they gave Syd a ride home. Stick and I helped Dotty clean up while

Joe sat with Caro in the living room in front of the fireplace. I stood in the entryway watching them—witnessing the ease and comfort they felt with each other, even after all the shit they'd been through.

"It's nice, right? Them?" Stick said softly behind me, watching the couple too.

"I guess," I said, not really sure.

We got the place cleaned up, and my father left, giving me a hug before he did. I thanked both him and Caro for the party. And, mostly, I meant it.

Stick asked for me to wait for him in the kitchen while he and Dotty helped Caro settle in for the night. I sat at the table in the nook area, where I'd spent so many afternoons drinking tea and talking with Caro—sharing her memories. Making some of my own.

"Ready," Stick said quietly as he came into the kitchen. He had a monitor to Caro's room in one hand and a bottle of champagne in the other.

"You know I only turned nineteen, right? Not twenty-one?" I said, rising from my chair and leading the way out the French doors and toward the guesthouse.

I heard Stick snort from behind me. "Please. The first time I met you, you asked me to buy beer for you. The second time, I had to drag you out of a club and you were too hammered to sit up straight in my car."

"Yes, but neither of those times were on Stratton estate grounds."

"True enough." We entered the guesthouse, and Stick turned the lamp on in the living area, but took my hand and led me to the bed. He sat down and I sat next to him, our hips touching.

"Now, tell me," he said. "Did we totally fuck up by throwing that party? Did you hate everything about it?"

I placed my hand on his knee. "No. Not everything. Getting stuff was cool."

He opened the champagne bottle effortlessly, without a drop of it spilling. He handed the bottle to me and I took a swig from it. It was cold and sweet, and the bubbles seemed to explode in my mouth. "Mmm, good. Sure nobody will mind that you took this?"

"I didn't take it. I bought it a couple of days ago, but kept it in the fridge in the house so you wouldn't see it in this one and get suspicious." I handed the bottle to him and he took a drink. "Okay, so, you gonna tell me why you hate your birthday so much?"

It was casual and he was handing me the bottle as he said it, but I knew he'd picked up on something. I wasn't about to ruin being alone with Stick and a bottle of good champagne by retelling the stories of the excruciating visits by Caro and her kids for my younger birthdays. "I could," I said, and took a small sip, keeping the champagne in my mouth. I leaned over, pressing my boobs against Stick's chest. He'd taken his suit jacket off long ago, and the tie was discarded while we were cleaning up. I kissed him and let the champagne flow from my mouth to his, our tongues tangling amidst the sweet nectar. "Or," I said, pulling away, "we could spend our time licking this champagne off of each other's bodies."

He studied me, seeing my diversionary tactic for what it was. He wanted to call me on it, I could tell. But then…he also wanted to do wicked things to my body.

"Fuck it. Tell me about your childhood scars some other time," he said, making me laugh. The gurgle of laughter had barely escaped my mouth when he'd started kissing me again.

It was different this time, because we had all night, not just some rushed time at the end of our afternoon visits. We slowly undressed each other, instead of tearing our clothes off, or even just working around them as we'd done on several occasions.

The champagne was used...creatively.

After the first time, we kept the lights on and explored each other's bodies slowly, languidly.

"I was shocked that first day, when you didn't have any tattoos. I would have thought for sure you'd have a bunch," I said as I ran my hands down his lean body.

"My dad said he'd kill me if I got one."

"Why didn't you get one after he died?"

"I didn't seem to need one then."

"Hmm," I said as I kissed my way down that ink-free torso. "Seems complicated."

"Isn't it always?" It seemed like he was going to say more, but I took him in my mouth and all he could do was groan.

Later, he returned the favor after he'd spent an inordinate amount of time kissing, sucking and playing with my breasts. It seemed as if he never got enough of them.

I totally got it, because it seemed as if I never got enough of him.

TWENTY-SEVEN

※

Jane

AMANDA TELLER was supposed to be the next Diane Sawyer. She was looking for that big interview that would catapult her into Katie/Diane/Barbara status, and so Grayson gave her our interview. I was guessing that he assumed she would be... *manageable* because she'd be grateful to get the gig.

She was, and it was pretty much a puff-piece interview, but I still felt incredibly uncomfortable.

Because, after trying not to my entire life, I was totally selling out.

We were shooting it in Caro's living room, with as small a crew as possible, and they'd all had to hand their cell phones to Elliot so there would be no photos of Caro—and her obvious decline—leaked before the interview aired.

At first they interviewed Joe alone. Caro and I sat in chairs along the far side of the living room. Stick and Grayson stood behind us, Stick leaning against the wall, his arms crossed over his chest, his dislike of my father obvious.

I was okay with that.

Grayson stood behind Caro, and occasionally she would wave him down and whisper something to him about whatever Joe had just said, or Amanda had just asked. Grayson would nod his agreement.

Much as I assumed they had in years past, they put their personal power struggle aside for Joe's benefit.

And my father had pissed all that away all those years ago by falling prey to my flighty, yet incredibly calculating, mother.

As if thinking about my mother had some kind of physical effect on me, Caro looked over at me like I'd twitched or something. Who knows, maybe I had.

She leaned over and said quietly, "Jane, you have told your mother about this, right? About your involvement in the campaign and especially the interview?"

No, I hadn't. I honestly didn't know how she'd react. One part of her would rejoice thinking about the time I'd be spending with my father, and how *she* could get in on that. The other part of her would totally lose it thinking of me spending time with Caro—putting forth a united front with the woman my mother felt was her nemesis.

She wasn't, of course. My mother wasn't important enough to my father to be Caro's nemesis, but she'd never understood that.

The problem was, I wasn't sure what part of my mother would show up when I told her about working on the campaign and going out on the trail this summer.

"Umm…" I couldn't outright lie to Caroline Stratton, but maybe I could hedge a little bit.

"You really need to tell her, Jane. She should not have to find out by watching Amanda Teller."

"When's the interview going to air?" I asked, trying to buy time.

"I'm not sure." She looked up at Grayson.

"Four weeks," he said with absolute certainty. I could tell by the way Caro sat up straighter, and moved a bit away from the back of her chair, that she didn't like that he knew something she didn't.

Four weeks. Four more weeks of pseudo-anonymity at Bribury. Four more weeks of not having to tell my mother. Four more weeks before my life as I knew it would change forever.

"But they'll probably start running promos for it in a week or two, once they make sure they've got all the footage they need," Grayson added.

Shit.

"I'm kind of surprised that Amanda Teller would do an interview for just a candidate for governor of Maryland. Seems like it would be more of a local news thing."

Caro looked over at me like I was a total newbie. Which, of course, I was, though I had picked up an awful lot about the political world in the last couple of months. More than I'd wanted to know.

"This is bigger than Maryland, Jane," Caro said, a bit of hurt in her voice, like I should know that fact. "*Joe* is bigger than Maryland."

Wow. All these years later, with the man's infidelity by-product sitting right next to her, she was still sipping heavily from the Joe Stratton Kool-Aid.

"Tell your mother, Jane," she said again.

"I find it interesting that you care about my mother finding out from someone else, about her feelings at all," I said to her, still speaking quietly even though my father and Amanda had wrapped up and were now out of the living room chairs and the crew was setting up for Caro to join them. "She certainly wouldn't care if you found out something the hard way. She wouldn't care about your feelings at all."

Caro looked off into the distance, out the side windows, and for a moment I thought she'd lost her train of thought. That was happening more and more regularly. That and her not being able to remember certain words; it was incredibly frustrating to her—a woman who knew her way around a thesaurus.

"At one time I wouldn't have cared about hers either," she finally said, turning back from the window, but not looking at me. "At one time I would have relished how she'd take the news." She took a deep sigh, then continued, "But I find that staring the grim reaper down has made me a bit more compassionate toward your mother."

"Yeah, that's probably what it would take for me to be compassionate toward her too," I said before I thought better of it.

She looked at me, shocked. After a second she burst into laughter, and I couldn't help but laugh along with her.

Stick

CARO AND JANE laughing over whatever Jane had said (and with Jane, who knew what that could be) was about the only truly honest moment of the whole damn day.

Caro and Joe were interviewed together, and the topics of forgiveness and second chances played a big part. As did Caro's illness.

She was forthcoming about her health and how much time she felt she had left. And damned if she didn't spin it to help Joe Stratton by saying things like dying had made her see what was really important, and it was the future for "our kids." And that Joe thought so too, and that was why he was reentering the political world—to make a difference.

Shit like that.

They really were something. Even in Caro's diminished state (mostly physical, but they did have to stop a few times because she had stumbled on some words), the respect and affection they had for each other was evident. And genuine.

At one point the interviewer asked Joe about losing Caro and never marrying again. I couldn't quite hear his answer, but it must have pleased Caro, judging by the look on her face.

Jane was added to the mix last. I tried to get her alone first. Not that I could give her a pep talk or anything, but just in case she wanted to vent or rage or whatever so she wouldn't lose it on camera.

But I shouldn't have worried about her. She was dynamic, with her father's natural charm, and the savvy she'd picked up along the road that had been honed by Caro over the past few months.

She was witty and sincere and talked about family coming in different shapes and sizes, and that everybody needed to look out for each other, and that was what Joe Stratton stood for.

She was magnificent.

But she wasn't Jane. Not my Jane. Not the Jane I held in my arms, or verbally tussled with. Or, hell, physically tussled with when it got real interesting.

We hadn't been together since the night of her birthday, when we'd spent the whole night in the guesthouse. And even though that had only been a few days ago, I missed it. Missed her.

Waking up with Jane, feeling her intense energy around me first thing in the morning, was more exhilarating than a triple espresso.

And certainly more arousing.

We took our time that morning, a slow, drawn-out session that almost had me saying words to her that I'd never said to any girl.

I'd wanted to that night, too, as I looked down at her, buried deep in her soft body. I'd almost told her that I loved her, but I didn't.

I could tell myself it was because I wasn't sure of my feelings, but that wasn't completely it, or at least not *only* it.

The truth was, I had no way of knowing how Jane would respond if I told her I loved her. I *thought* she felt the same way, but that didn't mean she would ever admit it. Jane would never show any signs of weakness, and I think she had some fucked-up logic that to tell me she loved me would be a weakness.

She wouldn't be wrong—she sure as hell had made me weak in some ways.

But stronger in others. And I was grateful enough to her for that to keep my mouth shut and not put her in a fight-or-flight moment.

"God, get me out of here," she said after she'd finished with the interview and come over to my side of the room.

I wanted to take her in my arms, hold her close, kiss the top of her head and tell her how well she'd done. But the crew was packing up while Amanda Teller spoke with Elliot and Grayson. Joe and Caro were still in their seats, their heads bent together. Probably planning how to take over Russia or something.

But, much as I wanted to, I didn't take Jane in my arms in front of everybody. She would have hated that. Instead, I said, "You were really great."

There was doubt in her striking green eyes, and just a tiny movement of the shield when she looked at me and said, "Really?"

Aw, fuck everybody else. I pulled her to me, and she only tried to pull away a little bit. I ran my hands up and down her back and whispered in her ear, "You were…fierce."

I felt her smile against my chest, and for just a second she relaxed into my embrace and her hand came up and rested at the small of my back.

But this was Jane, and in the next second, she took that hand and tugged at my belt loop at my back, pulling me away from her as she stepped back.

"Fierce? Like gay-designer fierce?" She said it with a finger snap and hand movement that looked, okay, yeah, just like a gay designer. Or maybe a diva.

I laughed. "No. Like you-are-not-one-to-be-fucked-with fierce."

She smiled. "Yeah, okay. I like that."

"You should. It's you."

I noticed Amanda Teller watching us with interest the same time Jane did. She took another step away from me. "I'm going to take off. I've got a class this afternoon that I wasn't sure if I was going to make or not. Looks like I'll be able to."

"I'll walk you to your car."

She went over and said her goodbyes to Caro and her father—hugging them both. I wasn't sure if that was for Amanda's benefit or not. Maybe not. Jane and Caro had grown pretty close over the past months, and she had even seemed to make strides with her father.

Jane was no dummy, and she knew she'd be spending a lot of time with him in public over the next few months. And if he won, and was truly back in the political world, it would be years. It was in everyone's best interest to bury resentment hatchets now.

At Yvette, Jane let me really take her in my arms and kiss her silly. In fact, she seemed to cling to me more than she ever had before.

"Was I really…fierce?" she whispered in my ear when we came up for air.

"Absolutely. Fierce. Fearless. Ferocious." I kissed her after each word, then went in for a long, languid tangling of tongues and mashing of lips. "Flawless," I added when I finally pulled away.

She smiled, and cupped my cheek with her hand, a very un-Jane-like move. After placing a gentle kiss on my lips she said, "Thank you for being here today. It helped."

Yeah, very un-Jane.

"Anytime," I said, meaning it.

She stepped away from me and got into the Vette. Leaning out the window, she said, "I may take you up on that." And I think she meant that, too.

The crew and Amanda Teller made their way out shortly after, the crew packing up their van and Amanda getting into a waiting limo. When I went back inside, Grayson, Elliot, Joe and Caro were around the dining room table, where they strategized for another hour. The dining room had pretty much stayed as command central ever since that day that Jane had joined them.

The day I took Jane's virginity. The day she gave it.

When the men left, Caro called me in to the dining room.

"Sit, Stick," she said, indicating the seat next to her.

My feelings for Caroline Stratton—much like my feelings for Jane—were incredibly complex.

I respected and admired Caro for the way she'd lived her life, the way she'd raised her children and for doing what she felt was the best thing for them even though it might not be the best thing for her.

But I also knew she was a shrewd woman who wasn't above manipulating people for what she probably considered the greater good.

I wasn't absolutely sure that her bonding with Jane hadn't been part of her master plan to help her ex-husband's campaign. And I knew she absolutely believed in Joe's destiny for higher office, and that it would only benefit her children in the end.

I wasn't sure she was right about any of that, but it wasn't my place to say anything.

Not that she would change her mind even if I did.

I cared for her beyond being her caregiver. But it wasn't as emotionally draining for me as doing the same things for my father. Yes, I had grown to like and respect Caro, but seeing her waste away was just very sad. Not emotionally devastating, as it had been with my old man.

The interview had taken a toll on her. She looked more tired than normal, even though she'd had her makeup and hair people in earlier today to get her ready for the interview. They even did Jane. Their phones had been confiscated while they were here, and they'd had to sign non-disclosure agreements, but Caro had wanted them here.

"You've got to be worn out," I said to her.

She just nodded and looked down at her hands, which were folded on the large mahogany table. I waited. She was at the point now where words sometimes escaped her. It had happened to my father too…at the end.

She took a deep breath, then reached out to put a hand over mine.

"I need your help with something."

"Anything," I said, thinking maybe she wanted me to carry her to her room or something. She really had gone past her limits today.

"I need to call Betsy and Joey."

"Sure, let me get the phone." It wasn't unusual for her to call them in the middle of the day. She spoke with her kids quite often, but hadn't Skyped or FaceTimed with them in a while, not wanting them to see her weight loss. I started to rise, but she put a hand on my arm, stopping me.

"It's time for them to come home."

TWENTY-EIGHT

❖

Stick

"SO, WHAT'S THIS all about?" I asked Lucas as he directed me
to park along the main drag in Pierpoint, a small, fairly affluent
town about forty minutes from Schoolport.

We were a few doors down from the hair salon where one
of my information contacts worked.

Back when I used to need information. I hadn't seen her
since the day I'd stopped by back in January, when I'd ended
things.

Both professionally and personally.

Shelly had taken it well—it was a casual, no-strings, not
very frequent hookup. She knew the score and seemed cool
with me cutting things off. Even thanked me for being honest
with her.

As honest as I could be.

Because it would have been way too weird to say, "Shelly,
you're great, and I really like having sex with you. But there's
this girl that I don't even like very much. And she can't stand
me. And, well, I don't think I can have good sex with you
anymore because I can't stop thinking about this girl…that I
don't even like."

So, yeah, I just said I was interested in somebody and I

thought it might lead somewhere and Shelly was cool.

"Is this about Shelly?" I asked Lucas now. I couldn't figure out why else he would have asked me to drive to Pierpoint.

He'd texted me earlier, saying he had something important he needed to talk to me about. Caro was meeting with Joe and Grayson, so it was good timing for me to be gone. When I picked Lucas up at his mom's place he just told me to drive to Pierpoint, not saying why.

We made small talk on the way, but I could tell something was bothering him.

"You don't need Shelly, do you?" I asked him now. "Like, you aren't…uh…taking over my action, are you?"

He gave me a "fuck you" look. "No. I'm with Lily. Completely. I don't need your old action."

I chuckled. "I didn't mean *that* kind of action. I meant the…car information action."

"Oh, right." He shook his head. "No, not that."

"But something to do with Shelly?" I looked up and down the street, seeing if there was any other possibility based on the businesses.

"Yeah," he said softly. "Listen, why don't you go in there and say hi to her. I'll wait here."

"Why would I want to do that? I haven't seen her in months. I don't *want* to say hi. Not that I have any issues with her or anything. It's just…over. It was never much to begin with. Nothing like what I've got with Jane."

Lucas took a deep breath, then let it out slowly. "Dude," I said, starting to get pissed off as well as worried. "What the hell is it?"

"I just think you—" He stopped abruptly, and I followed his vision. Shelly was coming out of the salon. She turned and walked away from us down the sidewalk. "Shit," Lucas said. "You need to go talk to her."

"Why?" I asked. But I had my answer as Shelly turned around, apparently forgetting something from the salon. As she turned our way, and then toward the salon, I could see that she was pregnant. Very pregnant.

"Oh, shit," I said, a feeling of dread easing over my entire body.

"Yeah," Lucas said. "I think you should—"

I didn't hear the rest of what he said because I was already getting out of my car and rushing to the sidewalk.

"SO WHY DIDN'T you say anything the last time we saw each other?" I asked Shelly.

She had agreed to meet after she was done with her shift, having just been on a break when Lucas and I saw her.

She seemed not at all excited to see me, but didn't hesitate much when I asked to talk with her.

I drove Lucas back to Schoolport, called in to make sure Caro was okay without me, then drove back to Pierpoint.

Now, Shelly and I sat at a diner a few doors down from the salon. She was eating a ham sandwich and fries, but all I had the stomach for was coffee.

"I wasn't sure I was keeping it when I last saw you," she said.

I started to say something, but kept my mouth shut, not really sure what I should say about that.

Not really sure how I *felt* about that.

"And the last time we saw each other, you were ending things, so I wasn't about to tell you then. It would have seemed like I was trying to keep you, trying to trap you."

"Shel, I know you wouldn't do that. We were always careful." Both statements were true. I'd known Shelly for a few years. She was a couple of years older than me and made an okay living cutting hair at the swanky salon. She wasn't looking for ways to keep me as a boyfriend. And we'd always used condoms.

"So, what was the plan? Were you *ever* going to tell me?"

She took a long time to answer me. Ate a few bites of her sandwich, took a gulp from her glass of milk. "Here's the thing, Stick," she said, then leaned across the table closer to me. "I'm not sure it's yours."

"Oh. Okay."

"I mean, I'm not a slut or anything. But let's face it, we were never more than an occasional hookup."

I held up my hand. "No explanation necessary. You were a free agent."

She nodded. "So were you."

"You're right," I admitted. There had been other girls in that stretch.

Until I danced with Jane at her sister's wedding. Then no other girl would do…even though I couldn't admit to myself that Jane was the one I wanted.

"So, obviously at some point you decided to keep it," I said.

A sweet glow came over her face. "Yes. It was scary as hell, but now…now I'm really glad and excited." She rubbed her hand over her huge belly. Over the baby.

My baby? Jesus, this was all so unreal.

"And when will we know if I'm the father?" I asked. "Some kind of test or something?"

"They have some prenatal testing you can do, but I'd rather not do the invasive stuff. There's also some prenatal blood tests they've started doing, but you have to send them off to a lab out of state, and it's expensive." She shrugged. "If you want, we can do a blood test after the baby is born."

"What do you mean if I want?"

She sat back in the booth, both hands now slowly caressing her tummy. "I intended on doing this on my own, Stick. I'm not asking for your help."

"I'd say that was obvious by the way you kept it under wraps. What about the other possibilities for the father? Do they know?"

She shook her head. "No. He's out of the picture, was before I knew I was pregnant. Like I said, I intended on doing this on my own. How did you find out, by the way?"

"Lucas saw you somewhere."

"Hmm. Yeah, I suppose something like that was bound to happen. With you being local and all."

"But—"

"I would have let you known. After the baby was born. I would have asked if you wanted to be involved. And I would have—will—if it's…the other guy's."

I believed her. Shelly had always been a straight shooter with me. And given the business we did together, there was a high level of mutual trust.

"How are you doing for money?" I asked. I knew the salon was one of the more expensive ones in town, but I couldn't imagine they had a good healthcare program. So she was probably on some low-priced, piece-of-shit healthcare policy.

Plus, she wasn't receiving the extra income I had been sending her way for information on her clients' comings and goings.

She shrugged. "It's fine. I'm fine." She wouldn't meet my eye as she said it.

"Listen, we'll figure it out, okay? I'm…I'm not going to let you go through this alone. I can help out financially with the hospital costs and stuff. I…" I knew what I was going to say. I also knew it was going to change my life forever. And that I was about to lose the one thing—the one person—who meant everything to me. "I will be a father to my child."

TWENTY-NINE

Jane

I COULDN'T BELIEVE what he was saying to me. I heard everything he said, but it was like the words were surrounding me in quicksand, and I couldn't find any solid ground.

We were sitting in Yvette, in Lot H. I'd met him there at our regular time even though he'd had to cancel the past two days.

Lot H. The scene of many a mind-blowing make-out session. And now Stick was telling me that he'd knocked up some girl.

I wanted to rage at him—totally annihilate him. But I didn't want him to know how much I cared. How much it hurt.

"Well, that sucks for you," I said. He just stared at me. I wanted to open Yvette's door, push him out of the passenger side, start her up and roar her to life and get out of this sucky parking lot. "I mean, I get it. We never discussed exclusivity. I'm just glad *we* were always careful," I said instead, in some breezy tone that I conjured up. Damn, now I really wished he didn't know that I'd been a virgin. I could pretend I'd been sleeping with someone else too.

And that thought—that Stick had been sleeping

with someone else (even though, yes, he had every right…
technically)—just about broke my heart. Not that I'd ever let
him know that.

He snorted in disgust. Like he had the right to show
disgust at what *I* said.

"That's not it. I've been faithful to you, Jane. It was
exclusive to me. I told her that I was out—casual as it was—
after that first day."

There were a lot of "firsts" with Stick. "Which first day?"

"The day I brought you Yvette. The day you told me about
you and your mom going to sit outside Caro's house when you
were a kid. The day you kissed the shit out of me," he said. He
smiled at the last, a sad, soft smile, and part of me thought that
maybe we'd make it through this. Weather this—baby-sized—
storm.

"There's only been you, Jane. Ever since that day. Before
it, actually. Since Betsy's wedding. I just didn't say the words
until that day. But I knew."

I'd known too, even though I hadn't admitted it to myself
at the time. Barely admitted it to myself now, after spending
nearly every afternoon with the guy for over the past two
months.

"And I *was* careful with Shelly. Every time. But, you
know…"

Yeah, I knew. Shit happened. And now Shelly was carrying
his baby.

Shelly. Stupid name.

He took my hand, held it in his on top of the console, our
fingers laced together. It was much warmer now, but his hand
felt like ice, and I bet that mine was just as cold. There was pain
on his face as he whispered my name, just staring at me. Not
leaning in for a kiss. Not trying to get me over the console. Just
looking at me.

The old me, the real Jane, would have pounced on his moment of weakness. Would have berated him for being careless (even though apparently he hadn't been). Would have used this moment to pull away from him and a relationship that could go nowhere even yesterday. Today, it was beyond impossible.

And yet I didn't do any of those things. Instead, I waited for him to say he wanted to try and make it work. For him to say yeah, it was complicated and uncomfortable, but what we had was worth seeing through.

But he didn't say that. And I...wouldn't.

He cleared his throat. I could see the struggle he was going through, and though I knew where it was all leading, I couldn't help but think about how handsome he was to me now. When, at first, I'd thought he was just ragtag and a little scraggy. Now, I saw the strength of his jaw, the determination in his face, the warmth in his brown eyes.

"I have to stand by her, Jane. I can't deny my own child. I won't."

Then. Then was when I fell in love with Stick Whatever.

He couldn't possibly know how much that particular sentiment, those particular words, would mean to me— someone who herself had been denied. Loudly and publicly.

Or maybe he did. Maybe he knew that was exactly what I needed to hear so that I could understand his choice.

A choice I knew he'd already made. A choice that would break my heart, just as I'd begun to understand its complicated ways.

"And...I just don't...want to be an asshole about this all. You know? I can't keep seeing you while somebody else is carrying my child."

"*Maybe* carrying your child," I said. "You said she wasn't sure." My voice sounded desperate, and I hated that.

Squeezing my hand, Stick let out a loud sigh, mirroring the heaviness in my own heart. "Yeah. *Maybe* my child. But we won't know for a while."

"And you want to put us on hold until then? Until after the baby's born?"

He shrugged, taking his hand from mine and facing forward, and I knew I'd lost him. No matter what I said, no matter what compromises I made. Me, who had fought compromise with both fists until a few months ago.

Until I'd agreed to be in the stupid wedding where I danced with Stick and he took my breath away.

"By that time your semester will be almost over. You'll be leaving shortly after that to go out on the trail for your father."

So, we'd always had a short shelf life? The duration of my freshman year? The life expectancy of…Caro?

I hadn't felt it was short term with us, and didn't think he really did either, but I didn't call him on it. "That's true," I said, not trusting my voice to say more than that. He looked over at me, as if he wanted to read whether what I'd said was true or not. I didn't look away. He sighed again and looked out the passenger window.

"So, how do you proceed with…Shelly?"

"I'm helping out where I can. She's got shitty health insurance, so I can help with the huge deductible. We've talked about her moving into my place, since it's two bedrooms and it doesn't look like Lucas is moving back anytime soon. She can save money that way."

I desperately wanted to ask which bedroom she'd be using once the baby was born. Or even before, for that matter, now that Stick wouldn't be sleeping with me. But I kept my mouth shut.

"Are you…okay for money?" I asked. I had no idea what Caro (or Grayson?) was paying him, but it couldn't be as lucrative as stealing cars. Which didn't seem to matter to him before, but now with another mouth to feed…and Shelly. Mustn't forget Shelly's mouth as well.

Plus, there would come a time—soon, apparently—when he would not be paid to be Caro's caregiver. Would he still continue working for Grayson in some other capacity?

"Yeah, I'm good," he said, still looking away.

"Promise me you won't go back to stealing cars for money. If you need any—"

"I won't. I'm done with that life," he said. "I was actually starting to look into going to nursing school." He glanced at me, but then away. I could tell he was kind of embarrassed about talking over his future plans with me now.

"Oh," I said.

He shrugged. "It was Caro's idea. She thought I'd be good at it. Home nursing in particular. I'd looked into it, but I don't know…"

"You would be good at it," I said with complete conviction. "I never saw you with your dad, but with Caro you're gentle and understanding, and yet you're tough when you need to be. You don't seem to be squeamish over the…gross stuff. And you seem to really grasp the medical part of it all. You're more than just a caregiver to Caro."

He absolutely was. I'd seen him set up an IV for Caro when she'd been dehydrated, and heard him discussing her meds and condition on the phone with her doctors. He'd come up with ways of helping her manage her pain, or if not, at least distracting her from it.

He shrugged again, looked backed out the window. "Yeah, well, that's on hold now. But yeah, I've got options. I can always work at my dad's old garage. It'd be okay pay."

We sat that way for a long time. Me thinking about Stick's future. Being a father, having a bond with his baby's mother, which would eventually blossom into more without me hanging around his neck.

I sensed (or maybe foolishly hoped) that if I'd made a case, he might have relinquished the no-seeing-each-other part. But to what end? Did I really want to be dating a baby daddy, always wondering what was going on at home with the baby momma?

No.

"One more thing?" I finally said.

He turned to me, and I could see his eyes were a little glassy with unshed tears. I thought about how much he probably hated that. Hated that I saw all that raw emotion from him. I would have hated it too, and said a silent blessing that I had enough of my parents' genes in me to be able to hide it.

"Anything," he said.

"You need to show me how to put the top down on this thing."

He let out kind of a half-laugh/half-sob and just nodded, already showing me how to do it, careful not to touch me as he leaned over and showed me the controls.

When the top was down and the March sun shone in, it felt like all our secrets had been given up to the light of day. Our past kisses in Lot H wafted away with the light breeze, as if they'd never happened. It smelled of fresh spring air, and I longed for the cold days where we could see our breath, and when we'd get close to each other and couldn't tell whose was whose.

"When you come to see Caro, I'll just hang out in the garage," he said.

I nodded. "I probably won't see her as much now with Betsy and Joey coming back." He'd told me Caro had told her kids the truth about her condition and asked them to come home. Betsy would arrive tomorrow and Joey later in the week.

"Don't let them stop you. I know Caro will want you to be there, while—"

"It's not my place," I said.

He gave a lopsided smile that didn't reach his eyes. "When has that ever stopped you?"

It would stop me this time. "We'll see," I said.

"Well…"

"Well…"

"Take care, Jane," he said, and got out of my car. The car he chose for me.

"You too," I said, turning Yvette on to cover the quaver in my voice. I drove out of the parking lot before he did. I knew he would turn left, so I turned right, not knowing where I was going.

I drove in a daze, but was so good with Yvette now that it was okay to be on autopilot. I took a country road away from Schoolport, but not in the direction of Chesney.

I found a deserted spot and pulled over. I grabbed the scarf and sunglasses Stick had given me from my backpack and put them on, tying the scarf around my head, then neck so it would stay on. Yes, very French-looking indeed. Getting back onto the road, I opened up Yvette, loving how the wind rushed past me with the top down for the first time. I shifted with ease, knowing the instant she needed to go higher. Needing to go there with her.

And thinking how much Stick would have loved it.

THIRTY

❖

Stick

SO THAT WAS IT. Funny, but I always figured it'd be the car stealing that did me in. And here it was a faulty condom.

And I was losing Jane instead of going to prison.

Not to be melodramatic, but that was its own kind of prison.

Caro began to deteriorate quickly. Betsy was by her side most of the time, and Joey too, once he got home. They both chastised Joe and Caro—and even Dotty—for not letting them know sooner, but I thought Caro knew what she was doing. She would have hated to have Betsy doting on her like this for the past two months.

I kept up with her care, but now that the interview promos would soon be running, more home nursing help came in. I watched and learned, and once again thought about doing this as a profession. I just couldn't figure out how to go to school with a kid on the way and all that entailed. If I could even get in to nursing school.

I didn't tell Caro the specifics, but she knew Jane and I were done. She didn't push, and I appreciated that.

The car collection was ready to be sold, if that was what she wished. It hadn't taken much, and really had been more of a front for me being there so often. She, Betsy, Joey and I went over the inventory list, me telling them how much they should list each car for, people I knew who might be interested…stuff like that.

I gave Lucas a heads-up that I'd need to sell my Camaro that he'd been using the past few months. I had a third car too, another Camaro that I'd restored. And, of course, my 1970 Dodge Charger. It would break my heart to sell her, but with the money from all three cars I could get one used, more family-friendly car, and still probably have enough to cover delivery costs and stuff like a crib and car seat.

I didn't let myself think too much about becoming a father. I was almost twenty-two. Younger than I would have liked to be when having a kid, but at least I wasn't sixteen or something.

I'd grown up without a mother, so I knew what would be missing from my kid's life if I left Shelly on her own, and there was no way I was going to do that.

There was no joy that I'd thought I'd hoped I'd feel when expecting my first child, and then I'd feel guilty about that. It certainly wasn't the baby's fault that I was in love with someone besides its mother.

It all just felt…numbing. Caro didn't have much longer. Jane and I were through. Shelly was due in four weeks. It was a lot of shit to deal with. But I did.

I didn't really have any choice.

Caro was in bed and the TV was on, though I didn't really think she was watching. I sat beside her, reading a book about cancer patient home healthcare. "Stick, would it be awkward for you to contact Jane and ask her to come see me?"

Yes, it would be awkward as hell. "No. Would you like me to do that?"

"Yes. I would like to see her. Soon. I know she hasn't

been coming because of Betsy and Joey being here, and that's probably for the best. But I would like to…"

"I'll let her know," I said, thinking I would just send her a text, then make plans to be away from the house while she was here. I didn't trust myself to hear her voice, or see her face. I had made a commitment to be there for Shelly. Not in a romantic way, but I just didn't want to have Jane's and my relationship thrown in Shelly's face while she was huge with my baby.

I don't know, it just seemed…tacky. Not that I was above tacky, but I was trying to be.

With no family in the area, Shelly had decided to stay in her apartment with her roommate until the baby was born, then they'd both move in to my place. Apparently the roommate was not keen on the idea of a crying baby. I knew how she felt.

"You know what, never mind," Caro said.

"You don't want to see Jane?"

She nodded, her head seeming so much larger now that her body was even smaller. "I do. But I'll have Betsy ask her to come."

My discomfort had probably shown on my face. "It's okay. I don't mind."

"I know. And I thank you for that. But it might mean more to Jane that Betsy asks her. They are sisters, after all, and they won't have me to facilitate their being together. Time for them to start now."

It made sense, but I couldn't help but wonder how Jane would take being summoned to the Stratton estate by Betsy.

But Jane, and how she felt, were not mine to worry about anymore. My choice, yeah, but it still sucked.

The promo for the Joe Stratton interview came on, and I tried to reach for the remote and turn it away, but Caro sat up a bit and slapped my hand away. Didn't have the strength of a baby bird, but she still had a pretty good swat.

"Wait, I want to see it," she said. We watched as the clip ran, random sound bites taken totally out of context to make the interview seem more...sensational, I guess.

"They moved the airdate from what they originally thought," she said.

"Did they?" I hadn't known the original date.

"Yes, it's two weeks later now." She was reaching for the phone, and I handed it to her. "Grayson," she said when the call connected. "Have you seen the promo? They bumped the airdate." She put the phone on speaker and laid it on her chest, the effort to hold it up seemingly too much for her. Must have been the hand slap that zapped her of any energy reservoir she might have had.

"Yes, they let us know they were doing that. Said it was because they wanted it to air during their sweeps week," Grayson said.

"Why wasn't I informed?"

Silence. "Honestly, Caro, I thought you wouldn't want to be bothered with something like that."

She gave me a look like, "can you *believe* this guy?" and I remembered Jane telling me that Grayson and Caro had butted heads more than once in the past. "Do you believe them? That it's based on ratings week?"

A pause from Grayson. "Maybe. It could also be..."

I didn't know what he meant, but it was obvious Caro did. "What's the biggest advantage to them?"

"I'm guessing they had the same discussion. Obviously they thought waiting would be the answer," Grayson said. "Am I on speaker?"

"Yes, but it's just me and Stick in the room. So, if I die before it airs, it's my last interview ever...that's a big draw."

"Right. But if you last until it airs, then they tout it as 'on death's door' or something. They'd probably rather have it...

after, but they can't wait too long."

"Or they run the risk that I give another interview to someone else."

"That would mess with our exclusive deal with Amanda Teller."

"But was the deal all-inclusive? Meaning, could just *I* give another interview? But the three of us together couldn't?"

"I'll check the language of the agreement. Are you saying you'd…be able to give another interview?"

"No, but they don't know that. Let's see what kind of leverage we need to control this airdate. We need to make sure it coincides…"

I didn't hear the last, making my way out of the room. She didn't need me right now—she was in her element. And honestly, I just didn't want to hear them strategize about how she could be a bigger asset—dead or alive.

This gig would be over soon, and I would miss Caro. And Dotty. And this house. But I would not miss the world they lived in.

The world Jane would now be a part of.

THIRTY-ONE

✦

Jane

BETSY SHOWED ME to her mother's room. Caro had been on the main floor since I'd started coming here, and I wanted to tell Betsy I more than knew the way, but I figured that would sound pissy. But that was kind of how I felt.

I couldn't help myself, but I hoped that Stick would be in the room with Caro. He wasn't. I should have been tipped off because his car wasn't parked out front in the large circular drive, but I figured maybe he'd begun parking over by the garage. Maybe now that Betsy and Joey were back he was acting more like…the help.

"Jane," Caro said when I entered her room behind Betsy. "Thank you for coming."

"Of course," I said, moving to the plush upholstered chair at her side.

She didn't look good. It had only been about ten days since I'd seen her, when we filmed the interview, but she'd declined quite a bit in that short time. She was propped up in bed, a thick robe wrapped around her frail body, a white nightgown peeking out at her neck. Her hair had been recently washed and was still a little damp. An IV was hooked up to one of her arms, and multiple pill bottles and paraphernalia were on the large bedside table.

There were fresh flowers in vases all over the room, and the window was cracked slightly, allowing a light spring breeze into the room. But even with all that, the room still had a… *sterile* smell to it. The smell of sickness. The smell of death.

"Can I get you anything, Mom?" Betsy asked, moving to the other side of the bed from where I sat down.

"No, thank you, honey."

"Okay, then I'll just leave you two alone."

Caro looked like she wanted to say something more to Betsy, but she didn't. Her eyes followed her daughter as Betsy left the room, closing the door behind her.

Thinking I was probably reading her mind, I said, "You can't force her to accept me, you know."

A sad smile flitted across her face. "Am I that obvious?"

I didn't answer that. "It'll either happen or it won't. You just need to let her make that choice."

She nodded. "But, are you…open to her if she wants a relationship with her sister?"

I took a deep breath. If my breakup with Stick wasn't enough, seeing this woman's life slipping away from her made me realize that you should never take any relationship for granted. "Yes," I said.

That seemed to satisfy her, and she leaned back against the headboard of the huge bed and closed her eyes.

I knew this would be the last time I saw Caroline Stratton. The last time to ask her some questions that I'd always wanted answered. "Why did you try to be a part of my life when I was younger?"

She didn't even open her eyes when she answered, "Because I loved your father, and you were his daughter."

"Even though he cheated on you? You still loved him?"

"Yes."

"And you *still* love him." It wasn't a question.

Only a nod from her.

"Was it…awful being around me when I was a kid? When you'd bring Betsy and Joey to be with me? When my mother would be in the other room?"

She opened her eyes, leaned away from the headboard. "No, not awful. Well, the situation was awful. Getting Joey and Betsy to go—and be civil—was awful. But it was important that they did, and I wouldn't have them do it without me there." She reached a hand out for me, and I inched to the edge of my chair to take it. "But *you* weren't awful, Jane. You were such an interesting person, even then. So smart, taking in the situation. Hating it, and yet…"

"Wishing I was part of your family," I finished.

She squeezed my hand, then let it go, leaning back.

"I'm in kind of a similar situation. I mean, the situation you were in back then. It has a lot of parallels."

She sat back up, with more energy than I thought she had. "Stick cheated on you? That surprises me."

"No, he didn't cheat on me."

"But you're not together?"

"He hasn't told you anything?"

She shook her head. "I could tell, but he didn't seem to want to talk about it. And then with Betsy and Joey home, and more home nursing people here, we really haven't had a lot of chances."

I told her the story. I felt kind of shitty doing it—it wasn't my place to tell her Stick had knocked up somebody. But it just seemed…right that Caro know. She'd been such an instrumental part of Stick and me even being together.

"And so you're wondering if you'll be able to accept Stick's baby like I tried to do with you?"

"No. I mean, it won't come to that. He ended it. I won't

have the opportunity to even see if I could…be a part of his life with the baby."

"Do you want to be?"

Yes. "I don't know," I said. "It probably wouldn't have lasted much longer anyway."

She looked at me for a long time, then leaned back against the headboard and closed her eyes. "You don't believe that. And neither do I," she said quietly.

I waited for her to say more, but she didn't. After a moment, I realized she'd fallen asleep. I sat quietly in the chair, watching the woman whom I, at times in my life, hated and loved, admired and feared, but always respected. Even when I thought she might be manipulating me, I respected her.

Because, at the end of the day, her motives were all about doing what she thought was right for her kids and the man she loved. My father.

I looked for Stick when I left, but didn't see him, and his car still wasn't in the front of the house.

When I got back to the dorm room, I sat for a long time and thought about Caro and the life she led. But mostly I thought about Stick, and whether I could be as big a person as Caro had been. If I could accept his child with another woman because I loved its father.

It didn't matter, though, because Stick wasn't giving me the chance to try.

Lily entered the room. "How'd it go?" she asked as she dropped her backpack on her desk, not really looking at me.

"It…it…" And then I lost it. Started crying. And I mean *crying*. Like, ugly hiccupping shit.

She was at my side in an instant, sitting next to me on my bed, putting her arms around me, rubbing her hand up and down my back. "It's okay. I know you thought of her…kind of like a mother. It's okay."

I remembered, not so long ago, that I had thought I would never cry about a boy in front of Lily like she'd done when Lucas and she had broken up. I knew Lily thought I was crying about Caro, and part of me was. But most of the tears were about Stick.

I let Lily comfort me, not even embarrassed that she saw me being so emotional.

For some odd reason, I thought about my mother. And the fact that I had one thing she never had—a best friend.

Three days later, I got the call from Grayson that Caro had passed that morning. In a weird twist of fate, I received a letter from her that afternoon that she'd sent two days earlier. She must have written it right after my visit.

It was on her monogrammed notecards; the handwriting was shaky, but definitely Caro's. It was only two lines.

His name is Patrick Dooley.

And he loves you.

THIRTY-TWO

❖

Jane

LATER THAT DAY I called my mother and told her that Caro had died. I also told her I had done an interview with Caro and my father before her death and that I would be involved in his campaign during the summer. She already knew that my father was running for office, of course, so them involving me wasn't a big shock for her.

I didn't tell her about spending nearly every afternoon for the past two months at the Strattons'. There didn't seem to be any point now, and I honestly didn't know what that information would do to her. The news of Caro's death confused her enough as it was. I could tell she was torn between wanting to call my father and giving him space. Probably trying to strategically play her cards. I was guessing she'd long seen Caro as the only obstacle between her and getting my father back.

She was wrong, but I knew she wouldn't listen to me on that score.

She offered to come down from Baltimore to "be with me," but I knew she just really wanted to go to the funeral. I told her no, that I was fine, and that I was certain the funeral would be private. She seemed to accept that, and I mentally sighed with relief, dodging the bullet of her making a play for my father while standing at the graveside of his dead wife.

Yes, ex-wife, but I knew my father still thought of Caro as his wife.

I wanted to reach out to Stick, ask him how he was doing, if he'd been there with her at the end. But I didn't.

I did tell Grayson that I wanted to go to the funeral even though it would be a private one. I thought I might have to negotiate on that one, assuming Betsy would not want me there. And maybe she didn't, but Grayson said right away that of course I would be on "the list," and gave me the details.

I wanted to pay my respects to a woman I admired. And, yeah, it was hard to admit, but I wanted to be there for my father too, who surely would be taking this hard, given their history and their…unfinished business.

But mostly, selfishly, I wanted to go just to see Stick again.

LILY WENT TO THE funeral with me, and I was grateful for the company. We drove out to the Chesney cemetery in Yvette, me in a tasteful black dress borrowed from Lily—who apparently had a closet full of them, because she wore one too.

When we parked at the curb amidst a small group of cars, I looked around for Stick's Charger, but didn't see it. Surely he would be invited to the funeral?

"He sold it," Lily said.

"What?" I said, playing dumb. "Who sold what?" But I knew. And I also knew why he'd done it, why he'd sold his baby.

For his other baby.

"Stick. He sold his car. And the one Lucas was using, and I guess he had a third one. He sold them all and got something different, something…"

"Kid friendly," I finished.

Lily had known Stick and I broke up, but I didn't tell her about his impending bundle of joy. Lucas must have. And bless her for not wanting to talk about it with me—I didn't think I could have handled it.

I looked at the group of cars, wondering if one of them belonged to Stick. It must have killed him to sell the Charger, he loved it even more than I had come to love Yvette. And that was a lot.

But he did it for the greater good. Much like why he'd stopped seeing me. Or at least that was what he'd told me.

We walked up the grassy slope, careful to mind our heels on the soft grass, to the area with a small gathering of people. Grayson came down and met us, giving Lily a hug and then even awkwardly hugging me. He escorted us up to the site and maneuvered us into the second row, where he had saved chairs for Lily and me next to him and Lily's mother.

I wondered about my being so close, if maybe I shouldn't move to the back, or even be one of the group standing behind the four or five rows of chairs. But my father was in the front row, just ahead of me, and he turned around and gave me a nod and a smile, so I stayed where I was.

It was a lovely service. After the minister spoke, Betsy said a few words, barely able to make it through, one hand clutching her notes, the other a linen handkerchief she needed throughout her eulogy.

Joey spoke too, and I could see both of his parents in him. A golden boy with his father's easy charm. He might abhor the limelight of the political world enough to give up his job and head to Africa, but if he ever changed his mind, he would make an excellent candidate.

My father was the last to speak. He was eloquent and charming and, I believed, totally genuine. There wasn't a dry eye in the house when he was done.

People started walking by the casket, still up on some kind of stage thing, hovering above the dug grave. Then they'd make their way past Betsy, Joey and my father and say a few words, or just shake hands. My father and Joey stood up for this, but Betsy stayed seated.

People were moving in an organized fashion from the back to the front, so we stayed seated in the second row until it was our turn. It was kind of nice, because I got to watch everybody else go through, hear what they said to the Strattons. A nice voyeuristic treat.

Until I saw Stick. I shouldn't have been surprised; I'd expected he'd be there, had even looked for his car. The car he'd sold.

But seeing him, and not being able to touch him, or throw a zinger his way, or run my hands through his messy hair—it was more painful than I would have imagined. I'd gotten pretty damn good over the years at pushing the bad stuff away, putting my shield (Stick's word for it) in place and letting painful things ping off of it.

But the shield was pretty thin on the day we were burying Caro Stratton, and what shred of it that was left was obliterated when he looked over my sister's shoulder and met my gaze.

He was wearing the suit he'd had on for my birthday party. He'd told me the next morning that it was the only suit he owned, that he'd gotten it for his father's funeral and hadn't worn it since before my birthday.

So, two funerals and a surprise birthday. Sounded like the title of a bad romcom.

He gave me a small nod, and I returned it, not trusting myself to do anything more. Moving with the rest of the line, he was soon behind me again, and I felt my lungs start to work once more.

Our row rose and moved to the end to get into the line. Grayson stood to the side, allowing his wife and daughter, and then myself, to go ahead of him. We moved slowly to the front.

Whoever was speaking with my father right now had pretty much stalled the whole process.

"So, it's over with you and Stick?" Grayson said quietly in my ear as he stood behind me.

I nodded and turned to face him. "I imagine that makes everybody pretty happy. No need to explain him on the campaign trail this summer."

He didn't answer for a moment, just nodded a tiny bit and looked thoughtfully at Caro's casket. "As a campaign runner, yes. As someone who has come to know the both of you? No, I can't say I'm happy about it."

I didn't have an answer for that, so I stayed quiet. We moved a few more steps ahead and then stopped again. Another chatty someone was with my father.

"You know," Grayson said, again quietly enough that only I could hear him, "Stick called me the night Lucas was arrested. After I'd talked to Lily. Apparently he was in the room when that call took place?"

I nodded. Yes, he had been. And I'd been there too.

"Well, he called me shortly afterward and asked if he could offer himself up instead. If instead of making Lily give up Lucas, I would give Stick to the DA in return for Lucas's freedom."

"He had mentioned that before. But we thought getting you involved was the better choice."

Grayson nodded, seemingly approving of what had been my idea at the time. I think in some sick way, he'd admired me for it. It was obvious now that he admired Stick just as much for what he'd done. "All this selflessness. From all three of you. Who says the youth of today only think of themselves?"

The line started moving again, and we were now in front of the casket, so I didn't say any more to Grayson. I knew I should be saying my farewells, or at least thinking about Caro.

But I'd said my goodbye to her in person, and this box in front of me did not symbolize the woman I'd come to know much better in the past few months.

Instead, I thought about what Grayson had just told me. I'd known Stick had a skewed sense of integrity. I mean, he was a car thief, but he also would have gone to jail for Lucas in a heartbeat. Had brought it up to Lily and me, and when I'd said we'd go with a different plan, he'd gone directly to Grayson to try and make the deal.

That must have been when he'd entered Grayson's radar. And Grayson Spaulding knew how to use people to their best advantage. And his.

And not just wanting to take the heat for Lucas, but the way he was standing behind Shelly, when he wasn't even one hundred percent sure the baby she was carrying was his. And selling his beloved cars to help out with expenses. How good he was with Caro, and apparently his dying father as well.

He called me fierce the day of the interview filming. If I was fierce, Stick was…ferocious. And loyal, and an all-around Stand-Up Guy.

I mean, I knew I was in love with him. I knew that I… *craved* him. But standing here, waiting my turn to pay my respects to my siblings and father, I realized I…*liked* Stick.

At that moment, I looked past the crowd and saw him at the very back of the gathering, watching me. I almost broke line and went to him, but before I could, he turned and walked away, disappearing down the slope of the hill, peeling his suit jacket off as he did.

Done with the world that required him to wear suits.

Find her. Be her…and let the rest of the bullshit go. Montrose's words played over and over in my head.

The rest of it—my father's campaign, Stick's and my different backgrounds and futures, him getting someone pregnant—while not insignificant, was indeed bullshit. And I needed to let it all go.

I needed him in my life. That's who I was. I had found her.

I was someone who didn't give up.

"We never did negotiate my continued involvement with the campaign," I said to Grayson.

I expected him to balk at that. Remind me of the car, tell me it wasn't the time or place to discuss it. "What's your price?" he said instead.

"I want Stick to be able to go to nursing school next year—if he wants to."

I waited for him to say he couldn't pull those kinds of strings, but he only said, "And?"

I smiled. The man knew me much better than my own father did. "And I want Amanda Teller's phone number."

He raised a brow at that, but didn't try to talk me out of anything, or ask what I intended. "And?"

"And you better start preparing some kind of spin, because I intend on making it work with an ex-car-thief who has an out-of-wedlock baby with another woman."

THIRTY-THREE

❖

Stick

THE ALARM ON MY PHONE went off and I put down the paintbrush. I was painting the second bedroom in my apartment a very neutral light tan. It hadn't been touched since Lucas had moved out, and I wanted to put a fresh coat on it before Shelly moved in, after the baby was born.

I enjoyed the mindlessness of it, the not having to think. So much so, I had to set the alarm to make sure I didn't miss the Stratton interview being aired.

I cleaned up my brushes and took a quick shower, and just as I was about to settle down on the couch with a beer, my phone buzzed. Jane's text tone. I debated even looking at it. I figured it was masochistic enough to even watch her on television, but to interact with her during it?

Curiosity got the best of me, and I reached for the phone, taking a drink of beer as I did.

Are you home?

Yes.

Can I come up?

Where are you?

Look out your window.

I was off the couch in a flash, and when I pulled back

the shades there was Jane, across the street, leaning against the Vette, phone in hand, looking like she didn't have a care in the world.

No care that just seeing her at Caro's funeral last week had been torture enough. I certainly didn't need her in my apartment—a place she'd never before been to. How did she even know where—

Lucas.

Stay there. I grabbed my keys and was out the door. Mentally making a note to let Lucas have it the next time I saw him.

She was at the door of my building when I got downstairs. "I was going to bring some champagne to toast and watch the interview with, but…my normal buyer wasn't available."

"What are you doing here, Jane?"

She moved past me into the vestibule. It was warm enough now that she didn't have a coat on, and she was only wearing what looked like a couple of layers of goofy tops instead of three or four. "Is my car going to be safe there?" she asked.

Typically no, but I owned this block when it came to cars. I walked a couple of steps out onto the stoop and looked around. "Ricky," I yelled to a neighborhood kid that was on his stoop a couple of doors down from where Jane had parked. "That car is with me. Under my protection. Anything happens to it and I will be very unhappy."

"Got it," the kid said. He'd make sure Yvette was left alone, and I'd slip the kid a twenty when Jane left.

Never mind that I hoped she never left.

She was already walking up the steps when I came back into the building. "Third floor," I called out, and followed her up, trying not to stare at her hips as they swayed underneath her flowy top.

Once inside, she made herself at home, sitting on the

couch, reaching for the remote. "You *were* going to watch it, weren't you?"

I shrugged. "I hadn't thought about it."

She narrowed those green eyes at me. "Yeah, right." She turned the TV on and flicked to the right channel. I offered her a beer and she took one, then I sat down on the couch, but not right next to her. She held out her beer bottle, neck pointed at me, to clink. "Here's to good television." I tapped the neck of my bottle to hers then took a long swig.

I was wishing I'd started drinking a lot earlier, because being this close to Jane without being able to touch her was something I really didn't want to do sober.

The interview was done well, but then I knew that it would be—I'd been in the room while they'd filmed it. Teller had asked Jane about family and how she felt about her dad and whether Jane thought Joe had integrity. Jane had answered pretty pat answers that she'd worked on with Grayson and Caro. But she didn't outright lie or anything.

She was just playing a part. Much like they all were.

I remembered that day so clearly—how I'd told her she was fierce and held her in my arms even though people were watching. How she'd let herself be vulnerable in front of me, if only for a second. How I was thinking I'd wished I'd told her I loved her on her birthday.

Now, it was a good thing I hadn't. It would have been that much harder letting her go.

During a commercial there was an awkward silence, which I filled by telling her something I hadn't thought I would get a chance to tell her. "Caro left me three of her father's cars in her will. Said she wanted me to sell them and use the money for nursing school."

"That's amazing. And not surprising that she would do that. She really thought the world of you."

I cleared my throat, a little embarrassed. I had been surprised to get the summons to attend the reading of the will. And then shocked to find out the value of the gift she'd given me.

"I was kind of surprised that she didn't leave something to you," I said. I had half expected to see Jane at the reading. "A piece of jewelry or something."

Jane shook her head. Her hair had grown since I'd brought her the Vette, now brushing her shoulders. "I wasn't. It would have hurt Betsy, I think. I know Caro cared for me, but at the end of the day, she wouldn't do anything that would hurt her kids."

I was going to say something to that, but the interview came back on and we watched the rest of it in silence.

"You were good," I said to Jane when the screen returned to Amanda Teller sitting in a chair back in the studio. "I thought—"

"Shhh, I want to hear this part." I raised a brow at her for shushing me, but just took another sip of beer and turned my attention back to the television.

"Shortly after Caroline Stratton's funeral, I received a call from Jane Winters asking if she could speak to me again. Here now is that conversation."

I turned to Jane, dread filling me. "What did you—"

"Shhh," she said again, adding in a hand motion this time. Her eyes were glued to the TV.

Oh shit, after Caro died Jane probably figured fuck it and decided to tell Amanda Teller exactly what she thought of dear old dad. Which was fine—I couldn't give a shit about Joe Stratton's political career. And in some ways Jane's life would be easier if his political ambitions bit the dust here and now. But I knew that to burn a bridge that large would put Jane in a major hot spot with Grayson Spaulding. One dude you did not want to cross.

"Jane, I understand you were at Caroline's funeral?" Amanda Teller asked Jane on screen. They were in a studio, and I wondered if Jane had gone to New York to do this.

"Yes, I was. It was, of course, very sad. But it was also a lovely celebration of her life. A chance for her friends and family to come together and share their stories and memories. Caro would have liked it."

Okay, so far so good. She wasn't saying "my dad's a douche" right out of the gate.

"And then you called me. Why is that Jane—what do you want to say that you couldn't while Joe and Caroline were beside you?"

Beside me Jane fidgeted, while Jane on the screen sat up straight, put her shoulders back and said, "We talked a lot about family and integrity that day. And at the time, they seemed like different topics to me. But now, after the funeral, they seem so intertwined."

Teller leaned forward, hungry for whatever scoop Jane was about to hand her. "How so?"

"Well, like in my father's case. Did he act with integrity back when he met my mother and I was born? No. And that cost him the love of his life in Caroline. Has he since tried to make it right and act in everyone's best interest? I think so. We all make mistakes. We all wish we could have a do-over."

"But don't you think integrity is at the very fiber of a person? That if you didn't have it then, you don't have it later?"

Jane pretended to mull that over, but I was willing to bet she knew exactly what she was going to say. "Not necessarily. In my father's case, I think it was losing Caroline that made him reassess his life and priorities, and from that came a new sense of responsibility, and integrity." Teller nodded, and was about to ask something else when Jane continued, "Like with my boyfriend, he's only twenty-one, but he has the strongest sense of integrity I know. Maybe not in some areas, but with the people he cares about, he would do whatever it took to help them out, even to the detriment of our relationship. He drives me mad sometimes, but I love him very much, and it's admirable, so I stand by him. And that's kind of like how my father…"

The interview went on for another minute or two, then went back to Teller alone in the studio signing off. I didn't catch what Jane said at the end, some kind of tying it all back to her father, but my brain stopped working when she said that she loved her boyfriend and stood by him. The screen went dark, and I turned to see the remote in Jane's hand, and her eyes on me.

Based on her expression—both apprehensive and curious—the shield was definitely down.

I knew how she felt—I had no defenses against what she'd said about loving me. My shield had been shattered. Had been shattered by Jane from day one. What she said wouldn't be a big deal to anyone else watching it. But to me? To me, she'd just given me the world.

"You added absolutely nothing to that interview in the eyes of everybody but me," I said cautiously. I didn't want the shield being thrown back up.

"I know."

"Why did she even run it?"

She placed the remote on the coffee table and took a sip from her beer. "She thought I was going to dish dirt. When it was over, she didn't want to run it, but I promised her first interview rights for the next three years if she aired it."

"You're kidding? And she said yes?"

Jane shrugged. "Nobody knows if Joe will win or not, but she probably figures if I'm in the limelight, then, knowing me,

I'll probably have some meltdown here or there, and she gets first crack at me. It was a risk she was willing to take."

"You will not have a meltdown. At least not so that anyone would see." I could see her flying off the handle when we were alone, ranting about something her father said, or Grayson did, but she would hold it together for—

And then it hit me. I was already seeing the future for us. Us. Together.

Jane

HE DIDN'T SAY ANYTHING more, and I sat very, very still. Like any sudden movement might scare him away. Slowly, carefully, I moved to the middle cushion of the couch, next to him.

"So, besides how I got her to run it, what did you think of the add-on piece?"

He put his beer bottle on the table and turned to me. "Nothing's really changed, you know."

"I have. I've changed." He quirked a brow at me. "Well, not really changed, but I realized what's important."

"And what's that?"

Screw slow and careful. I slid onto his lap and wrapped my arms around his neck. "This," I said in a whisper. Just before I kissed him. Of course he tasted like peppermint. And beer. And…Stick.

He kissed me back, his arms encircling me, pulling me closer. It would never be too close. Never close enough.

"Jane…I…" He was breathing heavily when he broke away.

"I love you," I said, trying to forestall any explanation about him and me being together being wrong while he was raising a child with someone else.

"I...I love you too," he said. Confirming my reason for being here. *Let the rest of the bullshit go.*

"We'll figure it out," I said, kissing him again, edging myself more fully onto his lap, already feeling him grow hard beneath me. "Who knows? We might break up next month. Next week, knowing the two of us." He gave a small laugh at that. "But we are *not* going to break up over this. Not over you stepping up and being a father to your kid."

"We're not?" he said, a bit of amusement, and what sounded like hope.

"No. We're not." A bit of my bravado left me as I asked the sixty-four-million-dollar question. "Unless things with Shelly have changed...for you?"

"Meaning?"

"Meaning, are you...together? Or want to be?"

He shook his head. "Nothing has changed with Shelly and me. We have not...reinstituted our...hookups."

I let out a of breath of relief.

"It's been only you, Jane. Since the start."

We made out some more. I wanted to get naked, but he seemed in no hurry, and I was totally enjoying the kissing, so I didn't rush it.

After a while, he pulled away again. "So you're sure? You're going to be able to deal with this if Shelly's baby is mine?" I nodded. "You are something, that's for sure. Not many girls would do that."

I thought for a minute, and then I conjured up the words Grayson Spaulding said to me at Betsy's wedding. "I have found it serves me well to see situations as they truly are, not as I would wish them to be."

He shook his head and took my face in his hands. "Who are you, Jane Winters?" he said, not for the first time. But unlike the other times, there was love in his voice, not exasperation. Okay, there was a little exasperation too, but mostly love.

"That's easy, Patrick Dooley." His eyes widened at my newfound knowledge, but I continued, "I'm your girlfriend."

EPILOGUE

Jane

Meet me at the hospital?

A text from Stick. I was just getting out of class, checking my phone.

Are you okay? I texted back, while walking quicker, my heart starting to beat quicker. If something was really wrong with Stick he would have called an ambulance, right? Not waited for me to get out of class and then text.

Yes. Just want you to see the world's cutest baby.

Oh, so Shelly had had her baby. I knew it would be any day now. My pace slowed down; I was no longer in such a hurry. I would love to get out of this, say I was busy and for him to go to the hospital without me. But Stick knew my schedule. I couldn't even claim to be heading to class. And I had told him I'd be supportive of him having a baby.

It had been three weeks since the night the interview aired, the night I went after Stick and told him I was going to be there for him—whether he wanted it or not.

Three weeks of figuring out how to circumnavigate this new world of ours, which would include me going on the road for my father this summer and Stick dealing with fatherhood, and starting school in the fall.

And three weeks of being loved by Patrick Dooley. That alone was worth all the other crap.

He had taken the money Caro left him—from the sales of the cars—and put a deposit on a second apartment in the same building as he lived. Even the same floor. That was where Shelly and the baby would come home to, not his second bedroom.

I knew it was mainly for my benefit, and felt bad about the money spent, but was happy about the choice he made. Lucas had even moved back into Stick's apartment now that Lucas's mother was doing well enough on her own. It helped with the rent, gave Lucas some space (though he still helped out a lot with his little brother), gave Shelly some privacy, but would allow Stick easy access to be able to help out with feedings and such.

The rest of the money he would use to go to school, looking at getting in somewhere within driving distance. He wouldn't let me use my negotiated chit with Grayson.

It just made me love him more.

I'd met Shelly Hopkins a few times over the past three weeks, and she seemed cool with me being with Stick. Even said another pair of hands for diaper duty would be great. Yeah, right. I mean, I loved Stick and everything, but there was no way I was going to do diapers.

Yes, it was all very civilized.

So why did I not want to go and see Stick's baby?

Would they name him Dooley? God, I didn't even ask if it was a boy or girl.

Hopefully I would fall in love with this kid right away and it would all work out.

"Hey, Jane. Got a minute?" Billy Montrose's voice pulled me out of my baby-induced haze. He was standing in the hallway of the building of my last class, in front of what I knew from my Montrose-hunting days was his office.

"Sure," I said, and made my way across the hall and into the office, him holding the door open for me.

It was a small room with just a desk, a bookshelf and an old leather couch, the kind that looked like you'd sink down when you sat in it, so that your knees would be at chin level. There were books all over the place, even some stacked on the floor beside the desk and couch. Stacks of papers were on his desk.

"The 'Who I am Right Now' papers?" I asked, pointing to a stack. It was the paper we'd had to write for our final for his class. The paper that had prompted him to give me the "Find Her" talk.

"What? Oh, yeah. Not as entertaining as last semester's batch, I'm afraid." He motioned to the couch, and I moved to sit down. His leather jacket was on the arm, and I moved it out of the way. Something dropped from underneath it and pooled at my feet. I bent over and picked up a beautiful, brightly colored scarf. A very unique scarf that I'd seen only one place before.

I held it to my nose. Yep, even smelled of her perfume. I handed it to Montrose, not saying a word, only raising a brow at him.

"It's, um…"

"Complicated? I'm sure it is," I said. He stood in front of me, looking down at the scarf in his hands like it held the secrets to the universe. Maybe, for him, it did.

Who was I to judge? I was on my way to meet my ex-car-thief boyfriend to see his baby with another woman. "Don't worry about it," I said to Montrose. "I won't mention that I was here…to anyone."

He nodded, still looking at the scarf. After a couple of seconds he gently placed the scarf on his desk, watching it, like it might slide off and away from him. Finally his attention turned back to me.

Funny, last semester I would have loved to have been given private attention in Montrose's office. Now, I just wanted to hear what he had to say and get out of there. And get to Stick.

"I saw the interview you did with the Strattons," he said. "And I was sorry I couldn't make it to Caroline's funeral."

That's right—he was college friends with Betsy. "It was a nice service," I said.

"I'm sure it was." He leaned against the front of his desk, crossing his ankles, and ran a hand through his wavy hair. Damn, but he was good looking in a tortured-artist kind of way.

And he did absolutely nothing for me. But I found myself happy that somebody was reaping the benefits of Billy Montrose.

"I just wanted to tell you...and I know this sounds kind of...*trite* coming from me. But seeing you in that interview? I was really...proud of you, Jane."

"Thanks," I said, meaning it. "Your words to me...they meant a lot. They really helped me out." I meant that too.

"I'm glad," he said.

I nodded at the scarf. "Now maybe it's time to take your own advice? Make it less...complicated? 'Let the rest of the bullshit go'?"

"Yeah, maybe."

I stood up, and we did one of those things where I went to hug him while he went to shake my hand, and it just ended up being awkward, but in a sweet kind of way.

I left his office, quickly walked to Lot H and took my baby to go see Stick's baby.

As we walked along the corridor to the maternity ward, my steps began to slow, nearly falter.

"Come on," Stick said, walking ahead of me. "You're going to love the little guy."

"Oh, so it's a boy?"

"Yep. Didn't I mention that?"

"No," I said. I didn't think he did. Stick had met me down in the lobby, and on the ride up the elevator he chattered about the delivery going well, and that Shelly's roommate had been in the room with her and came out to give Stick updates. And my mind went numb. He very well could have mentioned it was a boy and I'd missed it.

I joined Stick in front of the window with about eight babies behind it. Just like you saw in the movies. "There he is," Stick said, pointing to a bassinet just in front of us. The card in front of the bin read "Baby Boy Hopkins."

"Isn't he a cute little guy?" Stick said, watching me instead of the baby.

I took a good look at the baby, holding my breath in case he was the spitting image of his father. Which apparently he was.

"That baby is *very* Asian," I said.

"Yep," Stick said, still watching me, a broad grin creeping across his face.

"Does Shelly have an Asian background?" She was blonde and blue-eyed, but you never knew.

"Nope, not a drop."

"Do you?" Again, you never knew.

"Nope," he said, the grin growing wider.

"Are you even going to have blood tests done?"

He shook his head. "No need. A very bewildered, but mostly happy, Asian guy was here this morning. As soon as the baby was born, Shelly's roommate called him. He hadn't known anything about Shelly being pregnant. Apparently he's pretty happy about the surprise. I guess it was never his idea to break up. He's been with Shelly all morning. I think they might be working it out."

"So? You're—"

"Not the father? Yeah, that's pretty obvious now."

"And you won't—"

"Be involved? Probably not. I'll still offer to help out financially with the apartment if she needs help. But it's looking like the father is going to be involved, so it's probably best if I just bow out."

"And so we're—"

"Dealing with one less major issue in trying to make this thing called love fly."

I swatted his arm, my fingers brushing against the soft cotton of his white tee. "Would you let me finish a sentence?" He grabbed the swatting hand and raised it to his lips, kissing it, making my knuckles heat. Yeah, okay, making the rest of me heat, too.

I pulled it away from him and swatted again. "You couldn't have told me on the phone that he wasn't your kid? You made me get all prepared to see a Mini Stick and all those feelings to deal with?" Swat. "You can be such an asshat." Swat.

He grabbed my hand again and yanked me to him, wrapping his arms around me.

"Yeah, but I'm *your* asshat." He leaned down, resting his forehead against mine, gazing at me with those intense brown eyes.

I wove my hands behind his neck, entrenching my fingers in his rat's-nest hair.

"And don't you forget it," I said. Then I kissed him.

~*~

The Freshman Roommates Trilogy
continues with Syd's story in

IN TOO HARD
FRESHMAN ROOMMATES Book 3

Try Mara Jacobs's *New York Times* bestselling Worth series

Worth The Weight
Worth The Drive
Worth The Fall
Worth The Effort
Totally Worth Christmas

Find out more at
www.MaraJacobs.com

Mara Jacobs is the *New York Times* and *USA Today* bestselling author of The Worth Series

 After graduating from Michigan State University with a degree in advertising, Mara spent several years working at daily newspapers in advertising sales and production. This certainly prepared her for the world of deadlines!

She writes mysteries with romance, thrillers with romance, and romances with…well, you get it.

Forever a Yooper (someone who hails from Michigan's glorious Upper Peninsula), Mara now splits her time between the Copper Country, Las Vegas, and East Lansing, where she is better able to root on her beloved Spartans.

Mara loves to hear from readers.
Contact her at mara@marajacobs.com

You can find out more about her books at **www.marajacobs.com**

Printed in Great Britain
by Amazon.co.uk, Ltd.,
Marston Gate.